Murder by the Sea

A Mystery Novel by
Susan Evans McCloud

Bookcraft
Salt Lake City, Utah

All characters in this book are fictitious, and any resemblance to actual persons, living or dead, is purely coincidental.

Copyright © 1997 by Susan Evans McCloud

All rights reserved. No part of this book may be reproduced in any form or by any means without permission in writing from the publisher, Bookcraft, Inc., 1848 West 2300 South, Salt Lake City, Utah 84119.

Bookcraft is a registered trademark of Bookcraft, Inc.

Library of Congress Catalog Card Number: 97-71249
ISBN 1-57008-314-2

First Printing, 1997

Printed in the United States of America

This book is dedicated to
"Aunt Veneda" Curro,
who has nurtured me
and richly blessed my life

Chapter One

A cool sunset stretched thin and pale along the horizon. An obstinate breeze, with autumn in its breath, stirred the waters of the Thames into shivering peaks that spit a cold spray which the wind carried up the Victoria embankment. Callum MacGregor stood with his hands in his pockets as his men fished the gray sodden body out of the river and dumped it, like a great crumpled fish, at his feet.

What have we here, he thought, *at the very gates of the Temple?* He sensed the irony of the situation. Dead bodies did not customarily wash up in this neighborhood where the magnificent Templar church, begun in 1160, dominated the bank, with St. Paul's Cathedral, the National Gallery, and Covent Garden close behind; too proper and imposing a neighborhood for so benighted a visitor. He sighed and stuffed his cold hands deeper into the pocket linings. "Bring him aboard the *Chrysanthemum*," he instructed. "We'll have a proper look at him there."

The HMS *Chrysanthemum* was a sloop left over from the Great War, used now as headquarters for the Thames Division of the Metropolitan Police. Callum boarded her with practiced skill, pleased to find the small examination room warmed by the fire of a pot-bellied stove that stood in the corner.

"Name's Sammy Tableer," Callum's young lieutenant said as he entered. "Well known in drug circles."

"Wasn't he in on that warehouse heist last month?"

Terence Skinner nodded. "Small shrimp, this guy. Hardly worth the trouble of snuffing," he mused.

Callum arched a dark eyebrow. "So it may appear," he amended, a brusqueness thickening his Scots accent. "Someone thought it fit to make fish bait of him, now, didn't they?"

Terence nodded, thin-lipped. "Yes, sir."

Callum turned to examine the dripping contents of the dead man's pockets that had been dumped unceremoniously on the small table, which was covered, for protection, with a painted oilcloth. There was a half-empty pack of cheap cigarettes, a much-worn pocketknife, a leather purse holding the paltry sum of a couple of crowns, half a dozen bob, and a tuppence; and, not surprisingly, a crumpled, ill-used handkerchief. Callum poked at them distastefully with the tip of his writing pen. "Take these down to the station and file them," he instructed. "And let the crowner have a look at what's left of old Sammy. The cause of death is apparently the large knife slash in his chest, but the crowner might want to run an autopsy, just to be certain."

Terence nodded again, and turned to find officers to assist him. He did not see the chief inspector's pen slide a key out from under the hanky, pick it up with the tips of two fingers and slip it into his vest pocket. When he returned to the room to remove the body, Callum was already gone. The young officer shrugged; the big Scotsman had become a bit of a legend around Scotland Yard since the end of the war, and no one questioned his movements. He whistled to his mates and bent down to begin his distasteful task.

۞

Callum took the Waterloo Bridge over the Thames, then drove his black Magnette to St. George's Circus, where Waterloo intersects Borough. Off Borough Road is a narrow by-street called Gunn; he turned the car onto this poorly lighted section and shifted down into second, feeling his way nice and slow. This was not a detail he relished, but he knew traffic in opium and heroin which, put simply, was a drug produced from morphine, one of the active chemicals in opium. They were only now coming to realize how much stronger and more addictive this substance was; clinics were already being established to deal with the horrors of addiction. But it was the drug-related crimes that relentlessly escalated, from the jazz clubs of Soho to the warehouse districts, to the wharves where drugs and the staggering sums representing drug profit were smuggled in from all over the globe. Addicts would steal or kill for the fix they needed—a need that drove them to the point of madness; and beyond, Callum reckoned. But then there were those who were in it for the cold, hard profit; the worst of these being the legitimate doctors who catered to the opium eaters or heroin users, who would dangle "scripts" in front of their noses like bait, and play many a cruel game with the helpless and hurting.

Callum shuddered at the thought of it. He kept his hands firmly on the steering wheel, but his blue eyes, keen as a hawk's, were constantly moving, covering every inch of territory around him, over and over again.

In the years since the war ended the landscape of London had altered: both Barclay's and the Midland Bank had raised large, impressive structures in Picadilly; Fortnum & Mason had built a new neo-Georgian store, very tasteful in design; and the Devonshire House, which had started construction just five short years ago in '24, had become a vast commercial block, eight stories high. But here in the underworld, things never changed much. And for some reason he couldn't put his finger on, Callum liked that.

Leaving his car parked along the curb he got out and walked a bit, looking at ease among the costermongers, burglars and pickpockets, several of whom lifted their hats to him as he moved by. Some glanced askance, wondering if he had come to arrest them, watchful lest he avert that deadly eye in their direction. At length the inspector stopped in front of a low, dark structure, stuck his big hands into his pockets and, rocking back on his heels, began to whistle a careless air. After a moment or two the front door pushed outward and a thin shape, little more than a shadow in the gathering darkness, moved to stand beside him. They exchanged a few words, as vague and shapeless as their shadows. Then both moved away, parting as silently and swiftly as they had come together. The policeman walked back to his square black car, slid into the driver's seat and started the engine. With a sputtery growl as sharp and no-nonsense as a Scottish terrier's the car inched its way down the narrow, crowded street, patient and purposeful, until it turned once more and left the district behind.

᠅

It was full dark when Callum pulled up at the Mint, a well-known harbour for low characters of all varieties. He made his way quickly past the knots of men, four or five deep, who tightened their ranks protectively when he approached, and glared disapprovingly after him. He paid them no heed, but moved directly to a certain lodging-house, known as a haunt for thieves, and entered through the front door, ignoring the bold glances and ribald invitations from the painted-faced girls lounging there. He walked straight back through the unlit hall to the door he was seeking and turned the key in the lock, wedging it open only far enough to allow him to slip inside.

He gave a tug to the long gray string that hung from the ceiling, and the room, crassly lit by a naked bulb, sprung into view. Callum let his careful gaze travel the length and width of it, then he started systematically examining every inch of the place, emptying drawers, lifting rugs and cushions, even removing chair and table legs with a view to hollowed out places of concealment. "Dismal," he muttered to himself, his pent-up distaste transferring itself to the syllables. At length he straightened, rubbing his hands briskly against one another, as though to dislodge any taint that clung there. "Not a thing," he said, aloud again. *Dear heaven*, he thought, *what a way to live and to die.*

Then he saw it, the mere scrap of a paper stuffed inside the stove burner. He dislodged it from the others and smoothed it carefully. *A name and an address—not easy to read, is that a five or a seven? Little Surrey Street, not far from here.* The name was smudged over with coal dust. *Looks like M-u-r—Muriel; perhaps Millicent? A woman's name.* The last name was legible. Callum's face slackened with fatigue. *I'll check it out first thing tomorrow*, he thought. *Have a little light to see by then.*

He shuddered and reached above him for the string, plunging himself into a nest of darkness, close and dank, until his fingers located the doorknob and his means of escape.

Once out on the street he began walking casually, perhaps too casually, toward where his car was parked. Even in the darkness his eyes were continually moving, searching. A cat screeched and another answered it, and the lone inspector darted suddenly into one of the dark narrow doorways and pressed himself as close against the thin wood as he could. For long minutes he remained thus, part of the general murkiness that shifted over him. Two men had come out of the same lodging house he himself had just quitted. Coincidence only? Had they seen him enter Sammy's apartment? Callum shuddered at the thought. They walked within feet of his hiding place, but they did not slow their steps nor lift their noses to catch the scent of a peeler, a prowess they were wont to boast of. Callum remained as nondescript as all the other dingy street shadows until the two men returned, walking past him in the other direction; until he heard a car motor leap into life, and a long, impressive Bentley eat up the narrow street, then become a purring speck in the distance.

"What in the deuce was Logan doing here?" he muttered as he dislodged himself at last and took a few gingerly steps forward. Sammy was small fry; why would a man as powerful as Neville Logan personally concern himself with the likes of such street trash, unless . . . unless . . .

Callum reached the Magnette with a sigh of relief. "There is certainly more going on here," he told himself, "than at first meets the eye." The realization was not a pleasant one. It sat like the suggestion of a headache behind his eyes, like a ceiling of clouds above his head that made the dark night seem darker, crowded with evils he would not put a name to, even if he could.

༄

"Miss Millicent Symons?" Callum MacGregor stood at the door of the flat wishing he was wearing plain trousers and top hat rather than this symbol of authority which got in his way more than it helped him: a rounded "Bobbie" hat with a low, flat rim and a strap that wrapped round his chin; long coat buttoned up to his neck, with stripes on the sleeves and a Bull's-eye lantern strapped to his wide belt.

"*Miranda* Symons," the girl corrected with some hesitation, but with a look of purpose in her large, inscrutable eyes. Callum could feel curiosity pressing like a pulse against his temples. She was young, and as obviously out of place here, with her fresh-scrubbed face and country skirts, as a pint of cream is in a pickle factory.

"May I speak with you a moment?" he asked.

"If you must," she replied, staring at him as evenly and unflinching as any hussy with the design to disarm him.

He rocked back on his heels and coughed into his hand, attempting to portray a sense of discomfort. "Might I . . . ?"

"No. You can speak as easily from there as from anywhere."

Not one to waste either words or sentiment, Callum

thought, though there was nothing belligerent, or even disrespectful, in her tone.

"Are you acquainted with a man by the name of Sammy Tableer?" He was watching her expression, the muscles of her face carefully. "About thirty, thirty-five years old, little pip of a mustache, small eyes, set deep—"

Her eyes, looking back at him, were open and guileless. "I know no one in London, sir."

As his response registered disbelief, she continued, "No one save my friend Janey, who has secured me a job in one of the large clothing establishments."

"Two Cornish innocents working in a fine shop in London?" Callum couldn't help himself; the girl's composure piqued him.

"You are mistaken, I fear. You must have me confused with—"

"There is no mistake here." Callum pulled the crumpled bit of paper from his pocket. "This is your name and your address written here—and the same found in the room of a man who was brutally murdered last night."

Her eyes widened for the space of a heartbeat, that was all. She shrugged her shoulders and Callum realized that, though there was no spare flesh on her, she was not a small girl, but of a fine, ample build. "I cannot help you, sir. I know no more than I did a moment ago."

Yes, and I'll warrant that is much more than you are telling me! Callum rocked back on his heels and attempted to appear a bit menacing. "You do not find it unusual, perhaps even alarming, that your name was found in the possession of a known thief and street thug?"

"Was the dead man that?"

"Indeed, he was!" Callum growled. "And he had a mean twist to him, like the twist in his mustache." *Were the girl's cheeks blanching a little?* "It is of no concern to you what he was doing with your name in his possession?"

Miranda Symons shook her head slowly.

"I've no time to play games with you, miss. Whether you are concerned or no, the police, I can assure you, have a lively interest. What is the place where you work?"

The girl merely stared at him, her fine lips slightly parted.

"What is the full name of your friend?"

"I will tell you neither, sir, not until I have to."

Callum bristled, feeling perspiration gather under the line of his collar, "There is no need . . . you would be wise to cooperate." Now he forced himself to choose his words carefully. "If you have no friends in London, your life may well be in danger. Think well before you alienate your only source of aid or protection."

His fine words had not impressed her. Indeed, her eyes were more veiled now than when he had first knocked on her door. Perhaps he had succeeded at least in frightening her.

"Very well, as you will, miss. Until another time, then?" Callum touched his hat to her, and she moved the tilt of her chin just slightly in acknowledgement.

She is lying, he thought as he walked smartly back to his car. He disliked the role of bully; it sat ill with the gentleness in his nature—a trait he had never been successful in dislodging, even after his young wife died. He started the Magnette and drove toward the *Chrysanthemum* on the Thames, then thought better of it and turned above the Temple rather than below it, taking Fleet Street to the Cock Tavern, where Dickens and Thackeray used to take their ease and which still boasted the best glass of ale in town.

He sat there at one of the dark little tables which the autumn sun had not reached yet and wrote out his report. Head Commissioner Howe was a stickler; he would want all the details. He would want Callum's hunches, too. He chewed at the end of his pen as he sorted things out. Logan's presence meant that something big had gone down, or was about to. But how did the girl figure in? Not in a direct way;

Callum was almost sure of that. Somehow she had stumbled into a place where she did not belong.

He wrote carefully at first, then more hastily as the report stretched in length. He would recommend around the clock surveillance on the girl, at least for the next week or two. That might unearth any direct or accidental connections she had with the underworld, and perhaps serve to protect her at the same time.

Howe would have these papers on his desk by noon, and that would be the end of it, at least as far as Inspector MacGregor was concerned. Callum found himself wishing that the quiet, wide-eyed girl might be as easily out of the matter, as well.

Chapter Two

The call from the commissioner of police was not entirely unexpected; Callum knew Thomas Howe well. It had been three days since his conversation with Miranda Symons, but he had not been able to put the girl out of his mind. So he was not altogether unhappy to obey the summons when it came.

He found the little man sitting, gnomelike, in his big chair, waiting for him. "One hundred years, MacGregor, did you know it?"

Callum smiled. "That I do, sir. Eighteen twenty-nine—Sir Robert Peel, with some brilliant political moves and the tenaciousness of a tiger, established the Metropolitan Police Force."

Howe ran a restless finger along the line of his hairless eyebrows.

"But, remember, sir, the Thames Division was formed in 1798, the—"

"Yes, yes, the oldest, the best, the cockiest devils—and you foremost among them!" He chuckled at his big friend and rubbed his hands together in what Callum knew as real anticipation for the work ahead.

"Nasty business this. What think you, MacGregor?"

Callum was tempted to say, "You have my report, sir." But he let it pass and concentrated instead on what it might be that Howe wanted from him.

"Our government passed the Dangerous-Drug Laws nine years ago, and all that's really accomplished is to show us how mammoth the problem is—gruesome statistics; you know the sort of stuff."

Callum nodded and leaned a bit forward in his seat.

"Just last week the League of Nations approved the convening of a conference, worldwide, concerning this drug scene."

"Couldn't be hotter, then."

"That's right."

"Well . . ." Callum sighed and settled back again, a little hunch-shouldered. "Seems to me they're feeling their way still, not as well-organized as they'd like to be—depending on clumsy semiprofessionals who do messy jobs for them, because they have no choice—haven't set a higher calibre of men in place yet. It all takes time. But meantime the money is there, and greed overrides caution—sometimes even necessity."

The commissioner's eyes began to glint, and he nodded slowly.

"So men like Sammy get involved and complicate matters."

"Did Logan bump him off, or are we on the wrong track altogether?"

Callum arched his dark eyebrows thoughtfully. "Doesn't feel right, somehow. If Logan's men did him in, then what reason had the big man, himself, for poking around? I think it was something else—that hasn't yet surfaced."

"Yes. Well, the word is some large shipments are due any day now, goods worth millions of pounds, MacGregor, exchanged right under our noses!"

"It does rub, sir, doesn't it?"

The bright eyes narrowed, fixed the full extent of their energy on Callum's face. "I need you on this one, my friend."

"Can I not cover my end of things from the Waterfront?"

"I've already moved to increase the force there, as I have at other key spots. I need you here, there, and everywhere. I need you mobile, MacGregor!"

Callum frowned and the lines etched in his face seemed

more pronounced, like the scars of life which trace their paths along the countenances of all living men.

"I need your nose, man—your instinct! We're dealing with big money here, and big power of a type we're little accustomed to."

"Do you really think—"

"Yes. I believe you can make a difference, or you would not be here."

Callum grinned despite himself. "This was once considered the lowest grade stuff the Yard had to deal with . . . " He shrugged his shoulders. "I guess I'd best get that idea out of my head."

"I have before me a list of ten names," Howe began, not attempting to disguise the relief and delight he was feeling. "These are the odd cases, the long shots, the low-profile slippery eels that only surface now and again. Acquaint yourself with each of them—incognito on this, my friend—a shadow among shadows."

"And my lass from Cornwall?"

"Add her to the list."

"That's it?"

"Pretty sketchy, for now." Howe massaged his head, rounded and bald, with the tips of his fingers. "Report to me daily, report hourly, if you feel you'd like to. You have my private number."

Callum rose. "Yes. I believe I have everything I need, sir; at least at this point."

"Very good, my man. I am well pleased." The commissioner chuckled low in his throat. "But then, you already knew that."

Callum took the proffered hand, and the grip of the small, stubby fingers, whose power never ceased to impress him, closed over his own, reminding him of the brilliant mind and expansive spirit so well disguised by the inadequate physical exterior.

I'm in for it, he thought grimly as he stepped outside just in time to hear Big Ben chime the hour. Clear and full-bodied the repeated sound washed over him, perhaps incongruently lifting his spirits. He saw it not as the knelling of doom, but rather as a strong voice of hope that throbbed into every inch and corner of the city he loved.

༄

There was an officer on surveillance, but Callum went himself to question the girl. She stood as before, blocking the door as much with her presence as with her body.

"I know for a fact, miss, that you have not left these premises since the last time I spoke with you."

The ghost of a smile played around her mouth. "I have gone out twice to procure food, sir."

"Aye, a dozen steps from here to the street grocer. What of your position in the clothing establishment?"

"My friend was less than candid with me. It appears she cannot make good her promises." The broad Cornish accent did not mar the simple grace of the syllables as she pronounced them.

"You came all this way on the strength of a promise only?"

He thought Miranda Symons looked tired as she gazed patiently back at him.

"Then you are without employment, any means to support yourself?"

The obvious was there, she thought it unnecessary to respond to him.

"Your plans?" he pressed.

"My plans?" she repeated, as though slow to take his meaning. Then she lifted her head, a conscious gesture, and drew herself up, and Callum felt suddenly ashamed of his unseemly interference.

"Miss Symons, it is not my intent to distress you."

"I see," she replied, her mouth softening in disdain, not belief.

"I must warn you to do nothing hasty without informing us. In other words, do not quit these premises for any other; do not return to Cornwall without our knowledge."

"Our?"

"The police, the authorities. You take my meaning well enough, Miss Symons. I am not trifling with you; why do you insist upon playing the fool with me?"

His listener touched her fingers to her face, as though his words had stung her.

"Have I your word on it?"

"You have my word on nothing, sir." She moved, as she spoke, so that she stood a few feet inside the room from which the door now almost entirely shut him out.

"I am no threat to you," she said. "Nor can I help you in any way. Put your men to more useful purposes and leave me alone."

It was her coup. Anything further right now would be a waste of his time. Yet, her solemn words stayed with him. Alone in his own flat, eating his steak and kidney pie in solitude, he found them still running round his head. The obvious sincerity of them haunted him. And what, just what, if they were as truthful as they were sincere? Where did that leave her? Because Callum had no doubt that his strange, taciturn friend was involved with men and matters that posed a real threat to her life, and that, if known, might shed some light into the great cavern of darkness he felt he was wading through.

༄

Callum was putting the last of his washed and dried dishes into the cupboard when the phone jangled into life. He scooped the receiver up eagerly.

"Wilson here," the voice on the other end said. "Thought I'd best ring you, sir. Your little miss muffet has a visitor, a right handsome young fellow. Let him in the back door."

Callum felt the sudden increase of his heart beat. "Where are they now?"

"Sittin' in the parlor, nice 'n cozy."

"Don't lose sight of them for a moment, you understand me? I'll be right over."

"Yes, sir."

Action at last. A handsome young man. Callum tried to guess at the identity of the stranger; a futile exercise, but at least it was something to keep his mind occupied. Thirty minutes, if he was lucky, and he would be there. He knew a lot could happen in thirty minutes, but he would not let himself think about that.

༄

"Lost her? What do you mean, lost her?"

"Lost both of them, sir."

"That is impossible." Callum was not a man given to violence, but the drained, frightened face of the young officer maddened him. "Tell me what happened. Exactly."

"They moved into the kitchen, and it wasn't as easy to see them from the one high window in that room. But they sat down to the table—saw that with my own eyes. After a few minutes she drew the blind down, but I could still see them there. Just before you pulled up, sir, one of the bodies tumbled forward, all skitty-wampus like. When it stayed that way and the other one didn't move any, well, I began to wonder, so I found a box in the alley and stood atop it, sir, to peer in the window."

The man stopped and swallowed painfully. "There wasn't much light inside, sir, but it didn't look right. So I forced the door—" He moved back a step, as though expecting a blow. "They'd built up dummies with sacks and pillows, hats and scarves, even a wig, sir. I b'lieve it must 'ave been planned."

"And the door they used to make their exit was an inner door, you say, leading to the next apartment?"

The miserable man nodded. Callum sighed and patted him on the shoulder. "You'll learn such tricks yourself, in time," he assured him. "Who assigned you to this detail?"

The policeman hesitated briefly, realizing at once that his respite would be short-lived if the man above him got raked over the coals in his place. "Your man, Lieutenant Skinner," he replied uneasily.

"Terence! The young bloke has a penchant for jumping to the wrong conclusions," Callum growled. "Have you ever heard this phrase, lad, *never underestimate the enemy?* That is what has been done here. A slip of a girl, of little consequence—no obvious action—nothing but a daily tedium. Humor the old man and put a token watch on her. And then, suddenly, *this!*"

Callum's listener winced—*as well he ought to,* Callum thought, watching him. It was the inner connecting door that had been their undoing; in all candor, Callum, himself, had not anticipated that.

"I called for assistance before I left my flat," he informed the younger man. "I am going inside now to take a wee look around, carefully, so that, as far as our miss muffet can see, nothing has been disturbed. I'll cover the inside door; you and the others take care of all points exterior."

His eyes said: *Do you believe you can handle that?* The chastened officer merely repeated the two safest words he had in his vocabulary, "Yes, sir."

It was as Callum had expected; he found little to mark the girl's sojourn here. And more than tidiness was reflected in the order of her few things, she had taken care to be circumspect, as though anticipating . . .

Not until the second time through, searching pockets and hemlines in the few garments hanging in the closet, did he think to check the lining of the threadbare carpetbag tucked back in the corner. His fingers, stretching sightlessly, found and touched what they were after: a railway ticket, punched one way, but still good for a return trip to a certain town in Cornwall. He replaced it carefully, just as it had been before his intrusion and let himself out the front door.

A light mist sparkled, like bits of bright dust, under the shine of the street lamp. He instructed the little core of policemen, then stretched a bit and said casually, "I believe I'll take a bit of a stroll, lads, see what I might discover."

With that he set off in the direction of the pubs that lined the next street, one over. There were others taking the night air besides himself, but these were mostly in couples or small groups of mates. The only loners he saw were hollow-eyed men who passed him with hunched shoulders and downcast eyes. A pang of pity worked its way into his consciousness, more irritating than the moisture inside his coat collar, and his own loneliness seemed intensified.

I am lonely, he admitted, *and this life I lead will keep me that way. I deal in human misery, human fears and disappointments. I see the carnal side of man, glaring and piteous, and ofttimes forget altogether that he has a soul mixed in with the rougher stuff.*

He paused to let two women pass in front of him. One of them looked back and smiled. *Two women,* he thought. *The 'lovely ladies' I chased clear into Scotland, thinking I was on the trail of master thieves, while in truth I was hounding two very gentle, very innocent women . . .*

Thoughts of Laura Poulson and her daughter, Penelope, intruded like sunshine, piercing the wet pall around him. "How can I yet miss that woman," he muttered, "after nearly two years?" *Ah, but that had been a great adventure.* Indeed, as he had feared, life for him had never been quite the same since. *Times like that—people like that—well, they don't come along very often in one man's life.*

He reached a particular intersection and stopped, leaning against the lamppost, and pulling his hat down to ward off the thickening rain. Sounds from the brightly lit pubs floated out to him: men calling back and forth to one another, women's laughter, even the faint clink of glasses against the insubstantial background of a tinny piano tune he could not quite recognize.

Because he had not truly expected to see them, he nearly missed them altogether.

The girl was nearly as tall as her companion, who was well formed, but strung taut like a primed bowstring. His thatch of dark hair hung well over his forehead, and he kept pushing it out of his eyes. Even from this distance he was, indeed, a handsome brute, restless and brooding; certainly not her type. He felt an unaccountable stab of disappointment at seeing her with this dark one; in contrast she appeared more golden and serene than ever. Callum held so still that he realized his breath had caught somewhere back in his throat, and he had to fight a strong urge to cough and clear the passage again.

He was certain Miranda Symons had not noticed him. The two appeared to be arguing; his tone was as tight as the muscles along his stiff back and neck. Callum was good at detecting emotion where he could not catch words distinctly; a note of fear was unmistakable in the lad's voice. As he talked, she placed her hand with its long, well-formed fingers against his arm and began to rub gently, soothingly. *There are women,* Callum thought, with an almost detached observation, *who seem born with the natural skills of a mother—he had seen it surface in some of the hardest, most jaded women; he'd seen matrons who had raised large families and had not the slightest idea of what the word "nurture" might mean.*

But little miss muffet—why was she wasting it on this one?

She bent her head close to the young man's very suddenly, at the same time linking her arm firmly through his. Callum was hardly aware at first that they were moving away from him, so smooth and unhurried was the motion. With a wet swish a long black taxicab cut through the line of his vision. In a blur he saw the door open and the two young people disappear inside even as the tyres propelled the vehicle forward; one smooth, graceful moment, and in the space of a heartbeat they were gone.

Was she only lucky, or had she already phoned for a taxi, providing a sure escape, if necessary? Callum stared after, and was not surprised to see Miranda Symons turn around and fix her large eyes upon him; ageless eyes, as sad as the rain that streaked and blurred them.

She *had* seen him then but, with the poise of a professional, had not let on, had not in the smallest way tipped him.

Am I wrong about this girl? he asked himself as he walked back to the empty flat. *Is she so good that the innocent act seems real? Even the Cornish accent, could that be put on? Could I have bought a whole package, and not even known it?*

He felt tired and deflated. As he approached the little knot of policemen, so obviously wet and bored, he called out to them, "Go home, lads. Get some rest. We shan't be needing you here."

They looked up, their dullness startled. Only one dared approach him. He recognized Wilson's cautious face beneath the dripping hat.

"Would you like a couple of us to stay on, sir? 'Twon't be no bother."

"Thanks just the same, but it would be a waste, you see. Little miss muffet sat on her tuffet while she had to, but she's not coming back here."

"She's not, sir?"

Callum grinned. "Come out and say it, lad, say that you don't believe me. She won't be back, I tell you, not tonight, not tomorrow morning—not ever. Now, go home to your bed, lad, and that's an order."

He only hoped he could follow his own advice and put Miranda Symons out of his mind long enough to get the night's rest he was sure he would need.

Chapter Three

"They slipped through our fingers, old boy. We had triple the regular force out, yet the wharves may as well have been empty for all the good it did us."

Callum rubbed his hand over his face, as if to clear the thoughts that muddled and dulled his mind.

"You are certain your information was valid?" he asked the commissioner.

"No doubt whatsoever."

"They were obviously tipped likewise. All it takes is one man, sir, who knows well what he is doing—a solid wall of officers blocking all exits, and he still would have slipped through. Too many miles of dark, unguarded water, further obscured by the rain . . ." He let his voice trail away, as he was stating the obvious. "Did drugs and money change hands, you think?"

"Several times, I would guess. I look to see half a dozen foreign faces of ill repute around London during the next few days."

"How is that, sir?"

Commissioner Howe vigorously rubbed his bare pate. "What little we are getting from our street sources indicates that something has gone awry—what you hinted at the other day: inept agents, or perhaps a double crossing. Now, if last night's business involves the same parties, and things are unresolved still, I think we'll see some of the big bugs like Willis and Logan here overseeing operations themselves. I am relatively sure there is a French connection, and very likely an Egyptian, as well."

"So does Miranda Symons's disappearance with her strange visitor tie directly into this?"

"I believe that it does."

"You want me to find her?"

"If you please." Howe grinned at his own audacity.

"I have a hunch, sir. I do not believe she's in London still."

"Cornwall, is it? Well, that's coast, and heaven knows peppered with enough caves and warrens and coves used by smugglers for generations."

"And I am to step off the edge of the civilized world at such a crucial time?"

"It worked last time, didn't it, when I sent you to Scotland?"

"What if this girl's a red herring?"

"That is a risk we have to take. I do not believe that she is. I feel it in my bones, MacGregor!"

"Very well, sir. That satisfies me."

Callum rose to leave. "*Very* undercover on this, my friend. And no inexpedient risks. If it becomes necessary, there are those who can be sent at once to assist you."

"I understand."

"It is crucial, at least in the beginning, for no one to suspect that our attention has been drawn to Cornwall. If this has become a second field of operations, we want them to feel secure, free to move without risk."

Callum nodded.

"But if there is treachery, double dealing within the ranks, well, then things could become quite dangerous quite quickly."

"I will do my best," Callum repeated. "But, you know my ways, sir."

"That I do," the little man growled. "Both a curse and a blessing, you could be termed, my man."

The affectionate note behind the snarl warmed Callum's heart. On the strength of a hearty handshake he departed, wondering mildly if this was to become a pattern checkering the last years of his service: odd assignments which were a mixture of danger and boredom, requiring a high degree of efficiency as well as an element of imagination.

"Oh, sir, I am glad to have caught up to you."

Callum turned and regarded the red-faced Wilson, struggling to conceal his air of amusement. "What might I do for you, lad?"

"One last report, if I may."

Callum nodded.

"You see, sir, I lodged a card in the door of the flat last night before leaving. Then I returned only an hour past sunrise this morning to check it out." He drew himself up, as though about to say something very pleasing, or very important, or both. "You had the right of it. The card was yet in place, and nothing in the flat seemed the least bit disturbed, nothing missing, that I could see."

"Clothes and carpetbag still in the closet?"

"They were, sir."

Of course. The clothes could be easily sacrificed, even another ticket purchased, since expediency demanded it. Callum smiled. "Good work, young man. I admire your thoroughness."

Wilson worked hard not to beam his obvious, boyish pleasure.

"That, along with the pluck I've seen you exhibit, ought to take you far."

"Thank you, sir. I hope to be a credit to the force some day."

"If you truly want to, then you will be."

Callum walked on, thinking about his own youth: twenty seemed like a long time ago. He had willingly worked his way up from the lowliest street beat to a coveted position on the Thames Division, and this service as a plainclothes chief detective inspector that seemed to suit him so well. Despite his age, he still held an edge as far as skills and physical requirements for the force were concerned, and, somehow, his pride needed that. He could not be like the man he admired who had reached the top by dint of his mental powers alone.

"Would I even be here still," he thought idly, "if Annie had lived?" At times he doubted it. His taste for music and art and poetry was incongruent with the nuts and bolts of his work. He most probably would have taken a position in business and cultivated a lifestyle more in harmony with the spirit of the woman he had married. But, why think of such things now? No profit in it. She had been gone these long years, and was nothing more than a sweet memory—sometimes a longing—but nothing at all like reality.

Well, he thought, steering the Magnette along Bayswater past Kensington Gardens onto Palace Court, where his handsome row house stood, *another indeterminate stretch away from home*. He liked the comfort of his own things about him and his own reassuring routine. "That, if anything, proves you're getting old, lad," he said out loud to himself. Yet he had to admit to a building sense of excitement when he thought of the challenge which had been laid out for him. Change of this sort pared all the excess away from life and allowed the keen edges of the mind and spirit to show. *Maybe that's why I don't walk away from it*, he mused. The restlessness in his spirit which had been there since Annie left him, at least assured him that he was still alive.

He caught himself whistling a catchy Highland tune as he parked the Magnette and headed into the house.

༜

Miranda awoke early, as though, in some inner recess of her spirit, she could feel the sun on the water and hear the rush of the blue morning waves leaping up to meet it. *I can breathe again*, she thought as she quickly dressed. *I am home* once more. *All the smog and soot, all the ugliness of London is behind me.* She felt herself shudder as she thought of it. *Dear heaven,* she prayed, *let me forget the petrifying fear, the miserable helplessness, the sense of evil all around me.*

She slipped out the back door that led into the narrow yard bordered by wind-bent pines, and drew into her lungs the fresh, bracing air. She was struck, as she had been so often, by how fragile life is—and yet how tenacious. *I have both parts inside myself,* she thought, *so intertwined that it is impossible to separate one from the other.*

She walked slowly down the steep street that led from her house to Tintagel Road and Boscastle Harbor. She shook her long hair out, letting the sun seep into it, into her very pores, and felt cleansed by its fire and pureness.

Would it were so simple for Stephyn, she lamented. He had always been moody, even a little withdrawn, but since he came back from the war he had been different, and everything weak in his nature seemed intensified.

"There are wounds of the body, and there are wounds of the spirit," her grandfather had told her.

Yes, she knew about those. But that made it all the more painful to stand by and watch him, so helpless to do anything to soften his life! How could she have known? When he had come to her and asked what she thought about his going up to London at the invitation of his old army mate, she had thought it a good idea and urged him to go. *How could I have known?* she cried inwardly for the thousandth time, feeling the darkness she had been exposed to lunge out at her with its sharp fangs, like a hungry beast.

"Lady of leisure, is it, then?" The voice that called out to her was as warm and welcome as the sunlight.

"Oh, Bessie," she cried, "it is so good to be home."

"Big city life don't agree with you then, I take it, and you're ready to come back to work now, like the rest of us humble folk."

"That I am," Miranda laughed. She had worked half

days for Bessie and Frank Youlton this past year and more. They kept an inn and a little shop of sorts to the side of it. It was mostly a way to keep busy and earn a few pounds. Her needs were modest.

"You 'ave no ambition," her father was always growling at her. By this he meant that he thought she ought to go to Falmouth or Penzance, one of the bigger port cities, and find work, real work, and bring home wages. It stung her to know that he felt this way, that he had closed his heart to any role she might play in his life. He had not been thus before her mother's death. It was almost as though the very sight of her was too painful for him, and if she were gone and on her own he could forget about her. It was like him to think solely of his own needs; to be entirely unmindful of hers.

But she could not leave, not yet. She had made certain promises which she must fulfill. He was so willfully blind and selfish! She longed for his help now more than ever.

"Miranda, did you hear me?"

She looked up, focusing her wide eyes on the older woman.

"What a dreamer you are, lass. I said, you look a little peaked. Take advantage of this sun while we have it. The place won't fall apart if you be gone one more day."

"Thank you, Bessie," Miranda called, struggling to regain the feeling of peace and expectancy she had set out with. But the elusive moment was gone. She plodded on slowly, bracing her legs against the steep grade of the road, hearing only the seagulls as they cast their wing-spread shadows in front of the sun.

꒰

She knew she would find grandfather down in the inner pier just before the outer breakwater that held back the sea. He was tinkering; he was always tinkering with something on his boat or one of the others. He was a master at caulking, and had the patience for repairing nets and lines which some of the younger men lacked. He greeted her as soon as she came within hailing distance; he did not even look up.

"It is you, then, my dear, returned safely."

She smiled at the back of his head. Her grandfather's voice—cautious, reticent, nearly monotone—sounded older than his years.

"And how fares the lad?"

Miranda hesitated, longing to unburden her fears, but knowing how selfish that would be. At last she settled for a compromise.

"He is struggling."

"Struggling has ever been his way, hasn't it?"

"Aye," she sighed.

"Did he come back with you, then?"

"Not . . . yet." Fear began to spread through her, like some icy liquid poured into her veins.

"Tedn't one thing more you can do about it at present, my dear." He looked up from his work and his round eyes crinkled with kindness—"cozy eyes," Miranda had called them since she was a child.

"You are right, Grandfather."

"That's it. Get on with your own life and do the best you can—"

"What more can anyone do?" She laughed as she completed the phrase for him, but the words held their share of bitterness for her.

He does the best he can. That was the excuse the old man always gave her when she came complaining of her father. But she did not accept his generous assessment. No man could be so narrow and selfish who was doing the best that he could.

"I believe I'll walk on the cliffs a spell before breakfast," she said.

"Aye, you look a bit pale, Miranda. The sea air will do you good."

She kissed the back of his neck and continued on, taking the rough paths that veered to the left, meandering over the scaley rock surface where layer upon layer of purple-gray, brittle shale sat atop one another in fantastic patterns and forms. Indeed, the lines of the tide, itself, rough and irregular, seemed imprinted there, frozen in solid form.

Not for many minutes, until she had reached a great height, did she pause and approach the edge to look down. She settled herself on the windswept surface, hugging her knees, and watched the way the sun made the water alive, as though invisible fairies were dancing along the surface, each one a bright light—a bauble of water and sunlit air woven together—quivering with the very joy of existence. She sat for a long time, still as one of the gray rocks, as natural a part of the landscape as the rooks and the gulls.

The sea was not often thus. She would savor it as a hopeful omen. There was no harm she could think of in doing that.

ॐ

Callum drove straight through Surrey, Hampshire, Wiltshire, and into Devon, the heart of the Southwest. Here the wildness in the land became evident, and he felt compelled to take the somewhat longer, but scenic, coastal route, so he dropped down to Dartmouth, then over to Plymouth and across a rough inland stretch where the roads had no notion of what a tar surface was, to Port Isaac, where he picked up the coastline again. Here the A39 took him directly into Boscastle. The address he had scrawled from Miranda Symons's ticket had been copied into the back of the small book he carried, the same book which still bore the faraway desert address of the woman he had mistakenly hounded through the whole stretch of the British Isles.

Callum wore the coarse-grained, more loosely cut trousers of the laboring class, and a serviceable tweed coat to protect him against the sea winds of autumn. He still felt somewhat uncertain as to how his rough plan might work. As he drove he had sung every Scottish song he could remember, from the old Burns melodies such as "Annie Laurie" and "The Lea Rig" to the rousing war tunes like "Lock the Door, Lariston" and "Bonnie Dundee." He needed to feel at ease speaking with a thick Scottish bur, not the crazy quilt accent he had developed over the years, his own unique blending of Edinburgh town, the Highlands, and the London streets.

I can pull it off, he assured himself, remembering how well he had once played the part of an earl. He wondered, though, with no little curiosity, if Miranda Symons would recognize him, and what he might have to do to win her cooperation and trust.

꒰꒱

The first thing he did was simply drive round the place, slowly. Boscastle certainly had an air of its own. No tourist penetration here, but native men and women the sea had seasoned, and the roughness of the elements were built into the very houses themselves. Stark, one could call it, with white, slate-roofed cottages and shops hugging the colorless cliffs, or edging the long main street that followed the channel of the Valency River out to the port. Callum liked it, liked the air of honest toil about it, that spoke of people who knew what living was for.

He found a spot for the Magnette and walked into the Harbour Light, calling out heartily to the fresh-faced woman who greeted him, tasting the feel of the words, with the unaccustomed Scottish bur, on his tongue.

"You'd like a room, would you, this season?"

"I'm no' come as a tourist," Callum replied to the woman's keen words, and even sharper gaze. He tried to relax and make himself appear charming; however a rough

London policeman, unaccustomed to the company of women, did that. Then he thought of Laura Poulson, the American widow, and how easily he had fooled her into thinking him a Scottish earl. Surely he could convince this caustic Cornish woman that he was a gentle, ailing, middle-aged Scottish professor come to take the sea air.

"I've taught history in Edinburgh these past twenty-five years," he explained, "and my heart's been giving me a wee bit of trouble. Doctor recommended rest and sea air." He tried consciously to soften the aspect of his eye as well as the expression of his voice. "I chose Cornwall," he added.

"And why Boscastle?" the woman persisted, but her bristles had softened, and Callum thought he saw a real interest enter her eyes.

"Tintagel and Bodmin moor; this is unspoiled country, isn't it?" He smiled, and was pleased to see his listener's expression relax into a tentative friendliness. "I've a little research, a paper or two I'd like to work on."

She nodded. "Tedn't no better place for such, I reckon." She pulled the large guest book toward her. "You'd like a sea view, then?"

"Ah, that I would, ma'am."

While he wrote his name on the page she fumbled around in a large drawer and came up with a small iron key.

"You'll be staying for a spell?"

"Those are my intentions."

She handed the key to him. "Don't let this one often, but you'll be more comfortable there and have a bit more privacy."

"I thank you kindly," he smiled.

She glanced down at the ledger, then her eyes scanned his face again.

"Rory Forsyth. That sounds Scottish enough, I suppose."

" 'Tis, ma'am. My people go back to the time of Bruce and Wallace, and some even beyond."

"And did they come out for Charlie in the '45?" she asked.

"Some did, some didn't," he answered, marveling at how the history of one hundred years ago could remain such a real part of people's lives today. "You know how Scotland was then, kings and clans fighting each other for power."

She came near to smiling. "Aye, 'twas a rough time; I'd not like to have lived then. Violence everywhere, and not knowin' who you can trust when you walk down the street."

Callum tipped his cap to her and thought, a bit fiercely, *So it is now, my good woman, though the shadow of it has not yet crossed your path. Would to heaven I could prevent it altogether.*

"Your name again?"

"I never gave it to you." This time she smiled in earnest. "Bessie Youlton. Follow me, sir, and I'll show you the way to your room."

Chapter Four

Both men looked young for their years and, sitting as they were, companionably sharing drinks at the smoke-darkened inn, they appeared as nothing more than laborers relaxing after a hard day in the mines or the fields.

Stephyn, in fact, had just turned thirty in the spring, but his face looked youthful and tortured as he leaned close to answer his companion.

"Do you think me that much of a fool, Jean? I know the danger; I know it full well!"

"I do not believe so." The Frenchman was more cool in his manner, though his narrow eyes burned. "What you did in London was not only foolhardy, it was insane!"

"No one knows, not for certain."

"They suspect and, in this business, suspicion and fact are one and the same thing."

Stephyn took a nervous drink and swilled the dark liquid around in his mouth before swallowing. "I had no choice."

"You did!"

"I didn't!" Stephyn spat. "Thanks to you, friend, my choices narrow daily."

The Frenchman winced, as though the dark-haired lad had struck him. "I had no idea, not at the beginning—I swear it! I would never have purposefully involved you in such a nightmare."

Stephyn arched a black brow and glared at his friend. It was obvious that he did not believe the impassioned denial. "You knew more, far more than you told me." He hunched his shoulders, and the small gesture made him look both tired and vulnerable. "Me, what happens to me makes little difference. But Miranda—"

"She shouldn't have come to London!"

"I didn't invite her. I never dreamed—"

The Frenchman ground his back teeth together. "Be that as it may, she is still in danger, Stephyn. Does she know you are here?"

"Not yet. I told her I was going into hiding somewhere, and the less she knew, the better."

Jean Trudeau nodded. "They'll show up here in a day or two, and the game will be up."

"Not on your life."

"Stephyn, you can't hold out on them!"

"I can sell what they want at a price—"

"What price? Your freedom?"

"Mine and one other's."

"They don't *care*." Jean leaned forward, elbows on the table. "Why can't I get that through your thick skull? You have what is theirs, and they want it. That's all."

"But I am the only one who knows where it is. Not even you know that."

"So you think they'll bargain with you?"

"They'll have to."

Jean made a sound of despair, deep in his throat. "And you think they'll honor whatever 'arrangements' they make?"

"I shall have to be careful; get something in writing."

The Frenchman laughed out loud now, and the sound was hoarse and grating. "Give it to them, Stephyn, and be fair out of it!" he grasped his friend's wrist and forced him to meet his own burning gaze. "I mean it. You must do this; you must promise me."

Stephyn wrenched his arm away and buried his face in his ale mug. "I want my name cleared!" he said through clenched teeth. "I have no kind of future with a criminal record."

Jean Trudeau leaned back against the scarred wood bench and his thin frame seemed to go all loose and disjointed. They both fell quiet, and an air of despondency, as thick as the smoke in the room, settled upon them.

"Merciful heaven," Stephyn muttered at length. "I thought the Germans were unnerving. That kind of evil—when one knows exactly who the enemy is, and can have it out face to face with him . . ."

"My point exactly," Jean said, but he said it woodenly, and they both lapsed into silence again. After a few minutes the Frenchman rose slowly. "Give me ten minutes, fifteen, before you leave. And make sure no one follows you."

Stephyn answered without bothering to look up. "I'm in no hurry," he said. "I'm not going anywhere, am I?"

After his friend left he finished his drink and ordered another, and took his time with it. Nearly an hour had passed before he placed his money on the table and left the warm, dim room for the blackness of the moors. The thick yellow rays pouring out of the small-paned windows of Jamaica Inn were the only source of light in the inky atmosphere, and their fingers did not extend very far before the gloom swallowed them and the darkness became almost palpable. Stephyn stepped out into the darkness with a stride that was light and sure and headed at an angle across the wasteland, which was no more than a sightless stretch beneath the black sky. A person would have to know the pitch and roll of this bleak, scrubby moorland to follow where he was going. He moved silently, and after a few moments the shadow of him seemed to blink out and merge with the black rock and twisted bushes of broom he was moving through.

༃

Callum was pleased with his room and the aspect of the sea which its third-story location afforded. He slept well his first night, and felt an eagerness to be out and about, exploring the village and its occupants, seeing what he could see.

When he came down the steep, narrow stairs and followed his nose into the dining room, he was surprised at the breakfast laid out for him. A bowl of hot oatmeal and buttered toast had become his usual. Here were platters of thick-sliced ham, fried eggs, fried potatoes, turnip pasties, and oatmeal scones, still steaming. He made a glutton of himself, but he could not help it. It had been many long years since he had tasted the rich Cornish clotted cream that sat so well on a scone.

"All the sea air and exercise in the world won't help your heart much if you keep piling the cream on like that," Bessie Youlton scolded, coming up behind him. Yet, with a grin, she plopped another hot scone on his plate.

"I need a walk now," he muttered as he pushed his chair back and rose, a bit heavily.

"The morning's fair for it," his hostess assured him. "But take it easy this first time, and don't go tiring yourself."

Callum was more touched by her motherly concern than he liked to admit. He could not remember the last time a woman had fussed over him, albeit impersonally; it still felt amazingly good.

So did the cool air, which tempered the sun beating down on his head. He remembered hearing somewhere that the tanning quality of the Cornish sun was superior; a body could get a richer tan from one week in Cornwall than from three spent in Nice. The thought amused him; these serious, working folk had no notion of such indulgences; he would not like to be a bathing-suit clad tourist wandering down to the low wet ground of the Boscastle pier.

That was where he headed, along the narrow, curved path that hugged the layered cliffside, then veering right and sharply down the broad banked pier to where half a dozen men were working on crafts and netting.

He liked the smell of water in his nostrils; in this air the scent was nearly intoxicating.

The men at first seemed to take no note of him, save one old man who was varnishing a length of carved wood. He looked up from his work and squinted. "You be a stranger here, friend."

"That I am," Callum replied, feeling no pressure to speak loudly and brightly. In a few simple words he introduced himself and told his story, and the man accepted it so naturally that he halfway believed it himself.

"History teacher, is it? We've got history here in plenty."

This was precisely what Callum wanted. "When was this pier first built?" he inquired, by way of prodding.

"Built and rebuilt twice before 1584 when Sir Richard Grenville designed this one; him whose granddaddy died holding off fifty-two Spanish galleons with his one sweet little ship, *Revenge*."

Callum had heard of the Grenvilles, especially the ruthless Richard who fought so fiercely for the Royalists during the Civil War. "1584!" he marveled, thinking his own thoughts.

"Well, she had to be restored some in the mid-1700s. A good 200 vessels used to sail into this port each year, hauling out mostly iron ore—some coal and slate and timber." He shrugged his shoulders. "Now, after this confounded war." He rubbed a stained finger under his collar, then scratched at his beard. " 'Tis a proper shame."

"Yes, it is," Callum agreed. "So few messing things up for the lot of us."

The white-haired man grinned suddenly. "Hain't it always been so."

"Indeed it has," Callum sighed, thinking hard upon the tragic experiences of Scotland, trying to force the new, cruel drug lords out of his mind.

"Morris May be my name, sir." The man extended a strong, well-weathered hand for Callum to grasp. "That be my son-in-law yonder, Wilfred Symons."

Callum hoped his features did not register the elated

surprise he felt upon hearing that name. As he looked where the old man pointed, he saw a woman picking her way around the rocks and the damp, mossy patches to where Wilfred Symons sat with a length of netting. Callum watched the man look up and grunt when he saw her. Their voices carried to where he stood, but he could not make out their words. He noted that the exchange was brief, even curt.

"And who is the girl?" Callum asked, as casually as he was able.

"My granddaughter, Miranda. She be bringing her father his victuals. Pretty one, tedn't she?"

"Aye, she appears so."

"She'll save something for me, I'll warrant, and you can have the pleasure of a closer look then."

Callum noticed the warmth in the man's voice, and realized that all along it had been full-bodied and pleasant, with a singing cadence which was not unusual in those who had lived much of their lives on the sea.

Sure enough, Miranda turned and began to walk slowly in their direction. Callum felt a moment of panic. Would the girl recognize him? They had certainly stared, or glared, at one another long enough for her to have learned his features. Yet, his voice would be different, and his manner of dress . . .

He braced himself as she drew near and turned her large hazel eyes upon them.

"I've some pasties and mead here, Grandfather," she called. "But I did not know you had a visitor."

Callum swallowed, awkward still with his altered voice. "I ate enough at yonder inn to last me for two days. Came to walk it off, but I have not got very far."

"You will 'ave a bite, though, won't ee? No one makes pasties as light as my girl."

Miranda forgot to blush at his words. She was watching Callum intently. He hedged, not wanting her eyes to lock on his lest—

"This here be Mr. Forsyth from Edinburgh, dear. He's a professor of history in that place." Morris May sat on a dry spot of earth and turned all of his attention to the pasties.

"What brings you to Cornwall, Mr. Forsyth?" Miranda asked.

Callum recited his story for the third time, thinking, as he spoke, how very lovely her skin was and the sheen of her hair where the sun lent its brown tones the golden warmth of new honey. There was something not only quiet about her bearing, but stately, and she moved, he had noticed, with a willowy grace which belongs particularly to tall women.

"Have you been in Boscastle before?" she asked, after listening patiently. I have the distinct impression that you and I have met somewhere."

"I seldom come this far into England," he hedged. "Boscastle is new to me, and I must say it delights me already."

"He'd like to see a bit more of the place. Why don't you take him up on the cliffs, love? Every inch of this place—she knows it like few do."

"As you please, Grandfather," Miranda replied. But she turned and scowled upon Callum, so that her deep eyes took on a sad, almost shrouded glaze.

They took their farewells, Callum chewing on a bit of pasty and following the girl up the steep scaley slope at a pace that made conversation nearly impossible.

At length she slowed her steps. "There is a grand view from here," she said, "and a smooth place where we can sit down for a bit and rest."

She led him close to the cliff's edge where elderberries grew in profusion and the delicate pink and white blossoms of the sturdy thrift. He sat with her and admired the blue sea so far below, reluctant to spoil it all and plunge her once more into the nightmare that perhaps she thought she had escaped.

"Listen, Miranda," he began, "the truth is, you do know me; at least you have met me before."

"I thought so." The wariness was back in her eyes, and trembling in her voice.

"I am Callum MacGregor, the police inspector who visited you in London."

"Visited me? That is how you would put it?" A darkness clouded her creamy smooth features.

"My dear," he tried again. "I do not believe you understand what is going on here."

She leaned a bit away from him, turning her head at an angle where he could not get a full view of her face. "Tell me, then. I am listening."

He explained all he knew of the burgeoning heroin trade, the dead man's involvement, the emergence in London of powerful underground figures from several countries, the strong assumption that drug money, or large amounts of the substance itself, had been stolen, spirited away; double dealings within the ranks. She held very still and seemed to go pale as she listened.

"This kind of situation is most volatile," he pressed. "Things could get very ugly." He knew no way of telling her gently.

"And you believe these men are converging on Cornwall?"

"I am not certain, of course. But I am here to watch—to do what I can to prevent bloodshed and tragedy. Your friend, your dark, moody friend; we both know he is involved."

"He is not here."

"I would not take bets on that."

"He told me—"

"Miranda, really!"

"You do not understand." She passed her hand through her hair in agitation.

"Tell me all you know. Help me."

She turned large, miserable eyes on him. "I can tell you nothing."

"Your young man is in enough trouble that I could take him in right now."

"And yet you expect me to betray him."

Callum was growing frustrated. "You purposefully misunderstand me, young lady. I am here to help."

"You are here to do a job."

"I am here to prevent trouble"—he hesitated slightly—"and suffering."

She sighed and turned her gaze seaward. "I will keep your secret. That much I will do," she said slowly. "Beyond that, I must think about it."

"You have no time."

She did not deign to reply. Callum rose and paced back and forth along the edge of bare rock. "Your father," he asked, changing tack for a moment, "what kind of man is he?"

He thought she was going to ignore him again, it took her so long to answer. "He is a cold man. Life has disappointed him, thus he believes he has good excuse for disappointing life and ignoring its claims on him."

Callum was taken aback by her response and the emotion behind it, which Miranda was not able to cloak.

"Because he is a seaman, he is also restless, as well as weary of life."

"Your grandfather?"

"Yes. He has suffered full well as much as my father, yet there is no bitterness in him. He is a kindly man . . . patient."

"The sea can teach that, too."

She turned her eyes on him, warily inquisitive. "Yes, yes it can."

"I thought the old fellow delightful."

"Yes." She smiled wistfully. "He has cozy eyes, with crinkly laugh lines around them. And he has an insatiable curiosity."

"Well." Callum extended his hand and she took it and rose to her feet. "I shall not accept this as your final answer,

Miss Symons. And I hope you will allow me to pester you now and again."

Her thin hand, with its strong tapered fingers still rested in his. She regarded him thoughtfully. "I should like to think of you as a friend," she said, and her voice was low and richly-modulated, like the varied shades of the sea that swelled and echoed below them.

"I have a room at the Harbour Light," he told her. "If *ever* you have need of me—day or night."

"We shall see one another," she replied. "I work for Frank and Bessie half days at the little shop to the side of the inn."

Callum was pleased. "As they say in my country, 'ye ha a streak o' carl hemp in you.' "

"Which means?"

"You have an uncommon strong will and mind. You go with care, lass, you hear?"

She nodded, then stepped out ahead of him and led the way down the stark hillside. At the bottom Miranda took the path to her right, which would bring them into the town. But Callum hesitated.

"I don't think it best for the two of us to be seen companionably together."

She acquiesced. "I'll go ahead, then," she said, heading off. After a few steps she turned round to face him. "How ought I to treat you then, when we encounter one another?"

"Politely, if you can manage it."

His words drew a smile from her, a smile that lingered through the hours of his long, tedious day.

Chapter Five

The sun had set slowly, but now that night was scorching both sky and sea into blackness, the air had turned biting cold. Callum pulled the thick collar of his jacket up around his neck and tried to nestle his head in, turtle fashion. Heaven knew he had experienced many a cold night along the London docks, but it was different out here. Here the land, and the spirits of the land, took over once the light went away. Man was reduced to his primal condition of a weak, rather pathetic creature—no match for the elements that roamed at will over this wild, inhospitable space.

He walked along the town's main street, where the lights were thick and yellow. A thin fog was teasing its way over the narrow river. *Might prove nasty before night's end*, he said to himself. He found his way to the Napoleon, an inn that dated back to the 1500s. An excellent pub, he had been told at the Harbour Light. Here, if anywhere, a stranger in town ought to show his face.

He sat for awhile on a stool at the bar, watching and feeling, much as creatures of field and forest do when trying to scent their prey. When the three men entered he saw the difference at once. They were not dressed in the rough, well-worn work clothes of the other patrons, nor were their faces leathery tan and lined in patterns the sun and wind had drawn there. He turned at an angle where he could watch their progress. They moved swiftly to a corner table where two huddled on one bench and the third, a skinny stick of a man with hair too straight and long for his narrow features, stretched out across from them.

Callum was near enough to watch, but not to listen. So he observed how their mouths and hands moved, the tensing of facial muscles, small bodily gestures of anger or impatience. It seemed that the thin man was speaking a different language, but he could not tell what. So obviously out of place they were; he felt glad that he blended in as well as he did. After a while he thought he recognized the large, quiet fellow as one of the faces Thomas Howe had shown him, but he couldn't be sure. The man had dark blond hair, close-cropped, and well-chiseled features, but hewn from a hard mold; nothing soft or human-looking about him. The trio bolted two drinks each, in quick succession, then, moving like shadows, they left their table and started across the large, crowded room.

Callum rose, too. There was enough conversation and confusion that he was able to move unobtrusively at a careful distance behind them. But the gap, after all, was too far. By the time he cleared the big wooden door and stood outside the inn, the last of the three was climbing into a large, dark car that was already moving before he had the door closed. He watched after, disgusted. The vehicle made a sharp turn in the narrow street and headed toward Tintagel.

He took out his book and jotted down the number on the license plate. It would be fruitless to attempt to follow them, with the head start they would have. He'd ring London tomorrow. He scribbled a few more notes describing the strangers. Then he drew a deep breath and looked around him. How still and empty the night was, save for a restless wind blowing off the sea that was lifting the fog, so that it hung in the air like thin smoke now. Miranda had told him she lived up Fore Street in one of the fourteenth-century cottages the early seamen had built. Perhaps he'd go take a look at it.

He crossed on the first bridge he came to, a dark, humped stone structure that took no heed of his passing. Here by the river the fog had thickened. He turned up Fore Street and walked for a few yards. The incline was steep and somewhat tiring. As he slowed his steps he heard the distinct sound of a woman's voice. The wind carried it to him, like all the other whispers and shadows. He paused and listened, all his senses on edge. Where had it come from? It was difficult to judge for certain. He turned in the direction he thought and moved cautiously forward along the narrow, unfamiliar street.

※

The note was in Stephyn's handwriting. The blacksmith's young son had delivered it, and knew nothing whatsoever. What was he doing here when he had promised her he would go into a safe hiding place, which even she did not know of, and lay low for awhile? It grated to think that the haughty, handsome London policeman had been right, after all.

Meet me tonight, after nine. You know where.

That was all. Not much, if it had fallen into the wrong hands. In some ways she was anxious to see him, but she had carried a knot of fear in her stomach all day that had made her feel faint and sick. She was relieved when at last she could slip out of the cottage and down the hill to the dark cluster of trees and headstones.

She turned in at the gate, and did not mind how it creaked beneath her hand as she pushed it. There was no light here, the trees grew too close together; tall trees, bent with the weathering of ages, as tired and solemn as the graves they guarded. She moved among them with ease. Her mother had brought her here often when she was a child and told her the stories, the sweet tragic stories, over and over again.

The cold mist curled around her legs and tangled itself in her hair, but she paid it no heed. The spot she was looking for lay in the oldest part of the graveyard where the stones were so gray with age, so green with moss and lichen, that the names and dates were obscured entirely. Many of the stones were cracked or broken, some leaning at precarious angles, or reduced to lying face down in the damp brown grasses, nothing more than litter to decompose and decay.

Miranda picked her way carefully. Her mother's stone was one of the newest markers in this section, standing right next to the one for her sister, Florence, comfortably surrounded by a cluster of May ancestors. *Such a narrow, stingy allotment,* Miranda thought, *for men and women who were used to the wide open moors at their head and the wilderness of sea at their feet. Such a pity.*

She glanced around her as she walked. *He is not here,* she decided. *I would feel his presence.* When she reached her mother's grave she sat down on a rotting tree stump, prepared to wait patiently, at least for a while. The cold did not bother her: she wore two woolen petticoats, heavy shoes, and thick wool stockings, as well as the creamy thick Shetland sweater which had been her mother's. The mist—the mist distressed her a little. She always fancied she heard voices in it—sad voices, not wailing, but sodden with a blank and sightless despair. She hunched her shoulders against the mist and tried to think pleasant thoughts, but there was very little in her life that was pleasant just now. And here—here beside these two women who had loved Stephyn more than she ever could—here the haunting fears ate at her, like the gnawing of rats with their long sharp teeth.

After a few minutes she stood and paced the cramped space where movement was possible. *Where is he?* The panic inside her was building. *What could have prevented his coming?*

She cupped her hands and called out, and the gray air reverberated with the sound of her voice. She called his name, twice, three times, then wondered if that was a wise thing to do. *What if he was not alone? What if someone had followed him?*

"Hello, the kirkyard," she tried, making her voice sound as normal, as unstressed as possible. She repeated the greeting a second time, a third time, then she fell silent again.

"I will stay 'til the witching hour, if I must," she vowed aloud, her teeth clenched in determination. "He may be detained . . . he may be in need of me."

The words caused a hollow sensation within her, as though the world outside this silent place had somehow ceased to exist, and nothing mattered but her longing to see Stephyn emerge beside her—alive and well and part again of her own uncertain reality.

When she heard a step in the dried leaves her heart leapt and she moved forward in anticipation. But when the low-hanging branches parted to reveal the much larger bulk of the London policeman, she put her hand to her mouth.

"What are you doing here?" she demanded.

"I might ask the same thing of you," he growled.

"I live here! I've a right to go wherever my fancy takes me."

"To a graveyard in the middle of a night full of darkness and mist?"

"My mother is buried here." She spoke the words like an accusation, but he would not be drawn in.

"I am truly sorry for that," he said. "Now, who are you meeting?"

"I often come here to think things out, especially when my mind is troubled."

"Which I've no doubt yours is!" Callum moved a step closer. "Where is he, your dark-haired sweetheart?"

A mere wisp of a smile played along her lips, like a stray shred of the ghostly fog. "I do not know where he is," she answered honestly.

"Then he failed to show." Callum rocked back on his heels; she could feel the force of his pent-up energy reach out to her, and it frightened her a little.

"I am not a fool," Callum said patiently, as though

speaking to a willful child. "If you were not expecting someone, then who was it you called to?"

He had heard her, then! Inwardly cursing her foolishness, she gave the only reply she could think of. "I thought I heard someone coming; it must have been yourself."

"You disappoint me, Miranda." He spoke the words gently, softened further by his Scots accent. They shamed her more than any rebuke could. "Your friend is in danger, and so are you, my dear."

"So you tell me."

"Yes, well now I know of a certainty. The men we anticipated have appeared. That means our assumptions were pretty much on the money."

"You saw them . . . are you certain?"

"I have no doubt. Help me, Miranda! How long do you think you can be blind to this?"

She glared at him, her eyes like small glowing coals. With slow deliberation she moved and began to walk round him, but he jumped quickly to block her way.

"You are not safe out alone like this."

She raised her head with a disdainful air. "Not safe in Boscastle?" she mocked. "Step out of my way, sir."

"I could—"

"No, you couldn't. You have nothing 'on me,' as they say, nor on my 'dark friend,' as you call him. You don't even know his name, do you?"

Callum winced, glad for the cover of darkness. "Let me at least walk you back home."

"Leave me alone, else I shall set the local constable on you!"

Her low voice was trembling, and her eyes were wild so, with reluctance, Callum moved from the path and let her rush past. In a logical way he understood why she had lashed out at him; she was afraid and angry, and he was the only one upon whom she could vent her feelings. But it stung, anyway. As a man trying to do a dangerous, nearly impossible task, he found it difficult not to interpret her vehemence in a personal way.

Hazards of the trade, old man. The stock excuse leapt to his mind before he had time to think of another. Perhaps he was getting old. Perhaps. But it was not only that. He had been softer, more vulnerable since his encounter a year ago with the American woman.

He waited a few more minutes, then attempted to follow the girl at a distance, but she was already clean out of sight. *The impertinence!* With a long sigh he turned his steps in the other direction, and headed back to the Harbour Light and what creature comfort it might afford him.

༄

Miranda moved nervously through the dark streets. The damp air felt heavy in her lungs, and for the first time the shadows around her seemed sinister. With a scathing resentment she blamed that on MacGregor, or whatever his name was. She was weary and aware of a sense of abandonment, but she refused to give in to it. Foremost was Stephyn's safety. Yet she knew, with a prickling of panic, that it was out of her hands. She could no more control it than she could the swirls of fog that smothered and choked her as she pushed her way home.

༄

First thing the following morning, before all the shadows had melted or the dew had dried on the yarrow, Callum drove down the long, deserted road out of town toward the village of Tintagel. Only a few hardy farmers were out and about. He scoured the streets and the byways; the sleek black car had disappeared, like a fragment of last night's mist. He swore under his breath and went in search of a public telephone. It was too early for the offices at the Yard to be open, so he tried the commissioner's private number. After the first ring a cheerful, familiar voice answered.

"Thought it would be you, MacGregor. What have you got for me?"

Callum explained the events of the night before. He could almost hear the mind on the other end ticking. "So our hunch was right!" Howe gloated. "The unnerving fellow with the blond hair goes by the name of Gordon Willis. The Studebaker is no doubt registered in his name. It's a real favorite of gangsters in the States. Figures that Willis would think he ought to be seen in one. He and Logan, you know, are bitter rivals."

"Rivals?"

"Aye, always have been. But in international circles he carries more weight than Logan."

"So, who is double crossing whom?" Callum growled. "And what in the devil is bringing them here?"

"That's your job, MacGregor." Howe spoke the words in a no-nonsense manner, but the kindness Callum had learned to identify hovered behind the voice. "I'll check out the other one as well as the Frenchman, if you think that's what he was."

"'Good. Have you anything on Miss Symons's young friend?"

"Sketchy, too sketchy."

"I know. I'll just have to get more for you."

"Ring me tomorrow, MacGregor. I don't want things down there to get out of hand."

"Right, sir. Same hour all right?"

"Fine with me. Good hunting. Cheerio 'til tomorrow."

Callum replaced the phone in its cradle and walked back to his cold car and crawled inside. It would have to be breakfast as usual at the inn, to avoid suspicion. After that his first stop would be Webber's Garage, just on the chance that his strangers had stopped for services there.

❧

"Do recall a big American-make car coming through here yesterday, late. Three gentlemen driving her." The old man pulled at his full white beard.

"Did they stop, then, for petrol?"

"That they did." A younger man, overhearing them, stepped out from under the Mobiloils sign wiping his hands on a limp, greasy rag. "She was a honey, well-mannered for her size. Did you know the wheel base on the President—that's what Studebaker calls 'em—is 131 inches? Artillery duty wood on those wheels."

"Really." Callum grimaced, hoping his informant wouldn't notice.

"One hundred brake horsepower and five-inch-thick white walls, I'd swear. Do you know how fast she can go?"

Callum shook his head, resigning himself.

"They tested her on a course of two hundred mile, and her average speed was—you won't believe this—just over seventy-two miles an hour! Course, that engine . . . she be 336 cubic inches!"

"My Magnette is about a third of that," Callum admitted.

"Big American steel," the old man muttered.

"It do be intimidating!" his friend agreed with enthusiasm.

"What of the three men who were in her? Are they from around these parts?"

"Never seed 'em before."

"Big-city fellows; London written all over 'em."

Callum contrived to look slightly disappointed. "Oh, too bad. I saw the car go through here myself, and I've a friend back in Edinburgh has one. I was hoping it might have been him."

"Tedn't a chance. These blokes spoke the king's own English," the younger man assured him.

"Save for that long spindle-shanks. Sounded just like a Frenchy to me."

"Did you catch their names, by any chance?"

"Frenchman was Jean. The big blond guy turned around and said, 'Shut your mouth, will you, Jean?' when he thought no one was listenin'."

He stayed and chatted for a few more minutes, but the men had nothing of real value to give him, save this confirmation, which was really not necessary. Callum wished he could pull his credentials out and make compatriots of the two of them, but it was too early for that. He thanked them and left with what he hoped was the suggestion of a saunter. He'd call the Yard, a first name for the Frenchman might do something. Then he'd best get his books and papers together and play very seriously at being the odd-ball professor. His cover was important, very important, if he wanted to pull this thing off.

&

Rory Forsyth, Bessie informed Miranda, had already had his breakfast before she came in to work.

"Strange fellow, that. But pleasant. You 'ave met him?"

"Yes, down by the pier when I was taking my father his meal."

"Handsome he be for an older gentleman, with them fine brows and eyes that stare right through you."

"Yes, he is fine-looking," Miranda admitted.

"An' a gentleman—can tell from 'is voice as well as his manners."

"Bessie," Miranda tried to tease. "Could it be you're a bit sweet on the stranger?"

Bessie colored, delighted at the very suggestion. Then she leaned suddenly forward, lowering her voice. "Do you b'lieve he can be trusted, that one?"

Miranda swallowed. "I think so, Bessie. Why do you ask?"

"So many strangers around these parts lately; has my man a bit worried."

"Frank?" Miranda was a bit incredulous.

"Three strangers at the Napoleon last night; Frank saw 'em with 'is own eyes. Nasty-lookin' fellows, he says. Then, my friend, Nancy, called from Tintagel this morning. There be suspicious-lookin' strangers there, too."

"Maybe it's the same men."

"Mebbe. But I don't like it."

"We're spoiled here, Bessie," Miranda soothed. "We're used to our own ways, used to being able to name and greet every person we pass."

"That's right, an' that's how we want to keep it."

Miranda leaned over and gave the older woman a quick, affectionate squeeze. "Everything's changing. We'd best enjoy it while it lasts."

Bessie snorted disdainfully.

"I'm off," Miranda said, moving toward the door. "See you tomorrow."

"You watch yourself, lass. If any strangers come near you . . ."

Miranda tried to smile. She almost said, *I survived London, didn't I?* But the words stuck in her throat. Had she truly survived those nightmare days in London—had Stephyn? Or were they merely a prelude to worse things to come?

Chapter Six

Callum awoke to the wail of the wind outside his gray windows, as desolate, as desperate as the banshee who come after the dying to lead them away.

It had been a slow day, tedious and annoying, with the threat of a storm building and building; he could feel the labor of it as the long skies darkened and the gleaming seas churned. He had gone to his bed with the restlessness of the sea still moving in him. Yet, he must have slept, for the clock by his bedside read 5:20 A.M. He lay back against the pillows, but all his muscles were taut, and he felt a sense of disquiet that went deeper, even, than the rage of the storm.

When he heard voices, tense and muffled, a trigger within him clicked, and he rose and dressed quickly. *Something has happened,* he thought. Miranda's face rose up before him and, as it did so, a fear began to grip his insides.

He walked out of his room and down the stairs quickly, until he reached the floor level of the inn. At first the long hall appeared deserted, with no sign of movement or disturbance. Then he saw a sliver of light coming from beneath a closed door. With quick strides he reached it and knocked boldly. He could hear vague scuffling noises, then the door swung inward.

"Mr. Forsyth! Did we awaken you?" Bessie's voice was distressed and her face blanched white.

"The storm awakened me."

"Something right awful 'as happened." Frank Youlton spoke from within the room. Taking his words as an invitation, Callum pushed past his wife to stand beside the hearth grate where a warm peat fire burned.

"Ginger Fry and the Heard brothers, Peter and Louis, were out in their boats before first light–catch the dawn tide, you know, when the mackerel run."

"What did they see?" Callum was growing impatient.

"How'd you know they seed anything?"

"Your face is white as a sheet, man, and your wife is wringing her hands!"

"A small boat lying aslant the rocks, her bows pointed cliffward." Bessie's voice was shrill with unaccustomed emotion.

"There be a dead body inside."

With those words something in Callum was released. "Did they bring it in? Do they know who it is yet?"

"Couldn't. Ginger and Peter come back to get Alan Teague's big lugger. We're to meet 'em down by the shore."

Callum nodded. "Have the local police been notified?"

"The constable's Raymond Pascal over in Tintagel. He be visitin' his daughter in Penzance just now."

"I'd like to go with you, then."

Frank scratched his head and glanced at Bessie. "Suit yourself; you're welcome as any, I reckon. Can always use one more pair o' hands. Bess, have you got a spare slicker the professor can wrap himself up in?"

Bessie nodded and disappeared through the half-open doorway, returning before the two men reached the front door where a line of warm, hooded jackets hung on sturdy pegs.

"Take the biggest," Frank suggested, "and button up tight, sir. That and the slicker ought to keep you from freezing."

Outside the wind did not feel as fierce as it sounded, but it still buffeted them as they moved toward Callum's car. "How dare those men brave the elements on such a morning?" he asked the Cornishman as he rummaged through his pockets for the key.

"Rain's stopped, and this wind 'ill wear itself out before the sun's fairly up," Frank said, his voice as straightforward as his manner. "It be a small protected cove they were fishing, anyway. They saw the wreckage from there."

Callum drove the coastline from Boscastle to Hartland; wrecking country, where only the wild birds ventured the sharp-toothed cliffs and the sudden breathless drops from precipice to precipice.

At last he pulled off the road where his companion indicated and drove down what was only the suggestion of a path, until the undergrowth squeezed it too narrow for his Magnette to pass. He shut off the engine and stepped out into the night, all his senses keen, his eyes alive and watchful. He noted other tyre tracks beside his own in the wet earth, and several low branches were bruised and bent back, while others were cracked.

There was not much of a beach here, and the shoreline was littered with dozens of rock outcroppings, black and slippery with the continual spray that washed over them. He saw the broken-up boat, the white froth licking its sides and curling over its decks. In a small open space a body lay on a tarpaulin, with half a dozen men standing stiffly round it, one or two shining their torches over the grey, immobile features.

Callum pushed his way through until he stood at the dead man's shoulder. One of the fishermen glanced up at him and he heard Frank Youlton say, "This be one of those three strangers I saw in the Napoleon day afore yesterday."

"I do b'lieve you're right, Frank."

"Yes," Callum said sternly. "This is the Frenchman, whose first name was Jean." He realized that the silent men were all staring at him. "Old man at Webber's Garage told me that."

He bent down and rested on his heels, trying to examine the body with as little show of professionalism as possible. The others watched, fascinated, but a little put off, until Frank said, matter-of-factly, "Mr. Forsyth here be a professor of history in Edinburgh. He's doin' some research hereabouts."

The men mumbled and grunted, content with the explanation. At last Callum rose to his feet, knowing all he needed to know, but not yet willing to state it.

" 'Pears to me he was dumped in the boat yonder from some point up by the harbor and set adrift," one man offered, very much as though thinking aloud.

"Aye, and meant to wash out to sea, but the wind brought him here."

"Where the sharp rocks caught him and held him fast," Callum concluded. " 'Tis a pity."

"We'll lay 'im out in the church," Frank said, " 'til Peter's lad comes with the constable."

"A Frenchy." One of the men spat a cheekful of tobacco juice toward the line where the incoming seas chewed up the sand.

" 'Tis a proper nuisance that 'is friends come to Cornwall to do 'im in. Looks like a London kind of fellow to me."

Callum found himself agreeing, and remembering what was always said by the Cornish: *This isn't England, this be Cornwall.* Standing here among them, he understood how they felt. A *nuisance*; if he could only believe he might keep it at no more than that.

༄

He meant to find her at his first opportunity, but she found him.

"Who is this dead man?" she asked, her skin pale as ivory.

"He is not your young man," Callum answered her, looking up from the report he was writing. "Come with me."

Miranda walked with him to the stone church, its walls dark with lichen, its steeple standing like a faded sentinel against the gray sky that had never yet cleared. They entered together, though he stood back a little to let her pass first.

She walked with that measured gracefulness peculiar to herself, walked the long empty aisle with a determination Callum could not help but admire. For long moments she stared down at the dead man, so that Callum, waiting at her elbow, placed his hand on her arm. "What is it, my dear?"

She sighed deeply, and the sigh became a shudder that trembled over her frame.

"This is a damp, cheerless place for the dead to lie." Her voice was as hollow as the vaulted room where they stood. Callum led her gently to a side pew and sat down beside her. He knew, without being able to say why, that she would talk to him now.

"They were friends," she began. "Stephyn knew him from the war, from the time he spent over in France."

Stephyn.

"Do you think Stephyn knew that the Frenchman was here?"

"I am certain of it. It is this Jean who persuaded him to go to London in the first place."

"Persuaded him how?"

"Saying he was in need of Stephyn's help. I begged him not to go. From the very beginning I had an uneasy feeling—"

She paused and leaned forward, burying her face for a moment in the cradle of her outstretched arms. "But, what is there for him in Cornwall? Since coming back from the war he has been restless."

"That is not uncommon."

"Perhaps not. But we've no remedy for it, which other places might have. Did you know that bands of destitute miners who cannot find work roam over the moors in choirs singing for their supper, rather than digging for it?"

"I did not know that. What of the fishing?"

"Stephyn has no love of the sea—I think he fears it—which makes him, of course, a bitter disappointment as far as Father is concerned."

"Your father?"

She turned her great eyes on him, their brown depths wet with tears, so that they appeared like two dark, bottomless pools. "Stephyn is my brother."

Careful, Callum told himself. *Careful, lad.*

"You should have told me, trusted me, Miranda."

"And what good would that have done? You cannot change things that have already happened."

"We can alter the future." Callum's voice was warm with conviction, but the girl's eyes were still somber.

"Perhaps. To alter the future one must alter those who are to be involved in it." A wistful expression played at the corners of her mouth. "Even God seldom attempts to achieve that."

Where is Stephyn? Callum wanted to shout, shaking the solemn girl out of the melancholy which had seemed to come over her. Instead he said carefully, "Your brother, is he safe?"

"I have no idea! He told me in London to go home—that he had a good place to hide, and we both would be safe until the danger had passed."

"What danger?"

The muscles of her face tightened. "That I surely don't know. There are men, men with whom he is involved, thanks to Jean here. He is frightened, I know that. Perhaps he is trapped—like a seaman whose boat is caught in the sea when the tide changes."

"A foolish man." Callum bit his lip at having said it.

She looked upon him as one would look upon a very dim, very common child. "No, a seaman whose skill and daring push him to his limits, testing himself against elements few know how to harness to man's petty will."

Callum was silent. She had done this to him, but he did

not resent her for it, rather marveled at the strength and depth of her spirit.

"But it was your brother you were expecting that night in the graveyard?"

"He sent a note, brief and impersonal." As hope sparked in his eyes she added, "By the hand of a local child, who would know him, and think nothing out of the ordinary."

"Have you any idea where he might be?"

Callum saw the veil drop over her eyes; only a trained observer would have detected it. She answered him smoothly and naturally.

"No idea. We have never before had need to conceal ourselves—to run away—not in Boscastle."

"But this is wrecker country, from time beyond memory."

"Exactly. With more caves and warrens, coves and tors than could be discovered in a lifetime. Pick a place to start if you'd like, any place, and begin searching for my brother yourself."

She was tired of this conversation. She was tired of the wearing fear she lived with, day in and day out. Callum knew he dare not push her farther, at least not now. When she rose to leave he did not attempt to prevent her, did not speak the words he had intended to use to frighten her into cooperating with him.

Instead he stood in the chill, silent church, where the echoes of both dead and living seemed to mock him, and watched her walk away, with her head poised high, as though she were watching and listening for something which he could not see.

⁂

There was no relish to the next task that confronted him. He placed a call to Scotland Yard and asked one of the desk detectives to check on the name Stephyn Symons, spelled with a *y*. "I'll ring back in a couple of hours," he said.

When the phone went dead in his hand, he left the booth and drove back to Frank and Bessie's, to see what the local talk was, and to get a hot meal inside him. He felt chilled to the bone.

He was a bit disappointed. He had forgotten what a dour, independent lot the Cornish were. Used to rugged self-sufficiency—accustomed to stepping sideways of the law themselves when they felt justified—their biggest complaint was that the dead man was a stranger, and that his friends had chosen to do their dirty work here.

Talk over the bar and at the small, intimate tables had already shifted to matters of local interest: this man's cattle, that man's yawl, the fate of Wheal Coates, where some of the more fortunate miners still had jobs.

After considerable thought, Callum had made one decision: he would take this constable, Raymond Pascal, into his confidence; it seemed foolish to do anything less. If the Frenchman had died because he was unable to satisfy the demands of his tormentors—and Callum largely suspected this was the case, since the body had bruises and abrasions, signs of struggle, or even a pretty rough beating—if this were so, then Stephyn would be the next one they would go after. And they were angry now, their patience carried out to sea on the ragged storm wind. They would not bide their time much longer. Callum was certain of that.

The return call came late and the findings were just as he had feared. Stephyn Symons, it appeared, had been involved in several petty street crimes. But worse, his fingerprints had shown up in Sammy Tableer's flat, and it was the decided opinion of several that he was personally responsible for the murder. That chilled Callum in a way the cold sea winds never could.

The constable ought to be back, and it would be just as well to talk to him now, at his home, despite the late hour. At least the prying eyes of the entire community were not awake and agitated.

Callum drove the short distance to Tintagel, watching a dusky, burnished moon ride low over the water. A rain fine as mist wet his windscreen, but there was no wind. He had trouble finding the Pascal's whitewashed cottage, tucked in with a dozen others just like it. He rapped the iron knocker and heard the sharp sound reverberate. The man who opened the door to him peered squinty-eyed at the stranger.

"What do you want, friend?" he asked, but his voice was brusque and impatient.

"I know you have had a long, rather trying day, Mr. Pascal, but it is very important that I speak with you for a few moments."

"You be a stranger in these parts, and you 'ave the better of me, knowing my name, as you do."

Callum resigned himself, pulled his credentials out of his wallet and showed them discreetly to the constable.

"Well, well." Raymond Pascal was all whiskers, and now that he was smiling the effect was one of kindness and merriment. "Won't you step inside, sir?"

Callum followed his host into the room, almost stark in its simplicity and lack of the nonessential. But he could smell the warm burning peat, and a woman who must be Mrs. Pascal appeared from some back region with a steaming mug in each hand.

"This ought to do ee well enough." Raymond Pascal leaned back in his worn armchair, both hands wrapped round the hot mug. "Let us hear now what ee has to say."

༄

The man was more canny that Callum had anticipated, and too seasoned to think it merely a thing of curious interest that a chief inspector from London had come here in disguise. The import of all Callum had explained had sunk deep. Even the suggestions he offered were of an intelligent nature.

"I have men I can count on—both discreet and dependable. I'll tell them what they need, and no more." Pascal chewed on a ragged corner of his mustache. "I b'lieve it essential that you remain incognito, least for a while yet. You need the freedom of action, and my lads will be watchful—here, there, and where they are least expected!"

Callum could not help smiling. "I should like to find Stephyn Symons before it's too late."

"That will be the hard one. There we 'ave our hands full, for certain. There be dozens of places, over miles and miles of moorland, not to mention the rocks and the shoreline."

"I realize that," Callum agreed miserably. "But we must try—try as never before, man!"

"You 'ave my word on that."

Callum was beginning to enjoy the strange, almost singsong way the Cornishmen had of speaking.

"What be the name again—the name that ye go by?"

"Rory Forsyth."

"Edinburgh professor—and of history, no less." Pascal chuckled under his breath. "That be a good 'un."

The two men shook hands when they parted, and Callum felt comfortable with what had passed between them.

" 'Til tomorrow, then." He drove the black Magnette along the nearly-deserted road that connected the two obscure villages, wondering at the vagaries of time and fate which had brought him here.

Chapter Seven

The ruins of Bottreaux castle were covered over with centuries of earth and sealed in with a layer of tough green grass. Only the wall of one tower and a few crumbling remnants yet stood, stark and mute on the gentle slope above the city. Miranda found her way there as easily in the dark as she would have in daylight; she had traveled the same path, over the years of her childhood, many dozens of times. *Why did I not think of this earlier?* she chided herself. Although she was nearly twelve years younger than Stephyn, they had been close to one another, especially since there were no children in the family save the two of them. As he grew into his teen years he would often confide in her; she was a patient and sympathetic listener, and 'safe,' because she was so far removed from his own world, and a girl, besides. She loved him dearly; her mother had implanted that love in her, and Stephyn was as sure of it as he was of the tides in the sea. Love is a power. She had known, as she grew older, that her love gave her a power with him—the ability to influence him, even, at times, to help him. Then, he came back from the war, and their mother died, and he had no one, in his confusion and loneliness, but her.

Perhaps she was being foolish to think he would use the castle ruin, as he had when they were children. But, what other means had he? And a certain feeling had been growing in her . . .

When she saw the tattered Welsh flag stuck in the crumbling mortar, she put her hand to her mouth with a little cry. They had used the flag for years as a means of signaling one another; their father had brought it back in his ship many years ago. By now the red dragon had faded and the white and green background was gray, in places even tattered, from exposure to wind and weather. Miranda plucked it gently from its resting place, rolled it carefully, then tucked it beneath her arm. *If he had the flag,* she thought, *that means he was here in the village. But he did not try to see me directly, and must have thought this the only safe means of communication.*

She began to feel around the loose, chipped blocks carefully, her fingers pressing and probing. After a few moments she touched the creased fold of a paper and coaxed it triumphantly out. Quickly she moved to a sheltered spot beneath the shadow of the wall and, with a deep breath, unfolded the missive.

> Must see you. Come to the island—
> witching hour—please be careful.

The terse words were hastily scrawled, and they were not signed. She felt a hollow sensation in the pit of her stomach—not fear, not pain—more of a dull ache that stayed with her through the next hours when she patiently went about her ordinary business: feeding her father, cleaning the kitchen, banking the fire against the night, feeding the cats, sewing a missing button on one of her skirts. Once she heard her father snoring evenly from the next room, she could endure it no longer. She pulled a shawl from one of the pegs by the back door and slipped out into the night. She was ahead of the instructed time, but she would rather pace the high, brisk moorlands than wait, cooped up and stifled, down here.

She knew well the way to the lonely stretch beyond the small country church where Jamaica Inn sat, a brown dusky creature growing out of the very landscape. It was here the small, shaggy moor ponies, with their sweet faces, roamed in large numbers. She and Stephyn used to tame and ride them, and endow them with fanciful names. Thus, when they were younger and did not wish anyone—including their parents—to know where they were going, they would call the old inn *The Island*—for Jamaica was an island of the West Indies belonging to the British. How clever they had thought they were in those days!

The night air was cold, burning her lungs a little as she walked at a brisk pace. But the way was long, and she felt a terrible urgency to get there as quickly as possible.

She had just left the village behind and headed into the open moorland when she saw the yellow headlamps of a car trained upon her, and heard the grating whine of the brakes. She glanced around—more angry than she was frightened— to see the London inspector eating up the distance between them with long, hasty strides. She moved then, knowing she must reach the knoll a dozen or more yards ahead, where she could jump the frog stone, as they called it, and stand on the rise above him—away from the grasp of those iron arms.

He called her name out, but she paid no attention, concentrating all her energies on her progress over the rough, stone-littered ground. She could hear his laboured breathing behind her, encouraged that he found the course strenuous. At length, when she reached her small promontory, she whirled quickly round.

"Leave me alone!" she screamed. She bent and scooped up a large stone and held it, with both hands, above her head.

He paused, uncertain for a moment. But then he switched on the torch he carried and trained it on her face, so that the bright light would blind her.

"I did not take you for such a foolish girl, Miranda," he called out. "I know you are going to meet Stephyn. Let me come with you; you dare not go alone."

His words maddened her. *You dare not!* Who was he to address her in such a way?

"For heaven's sake, lass, I can protect the both of you."

She did not think so. He was, after all a policeman with a duty to perform. His duty would bind him to taking Stephyn into custody, and she knew her brother would never allow that. She *must* talk to him first, alone; she owed him at least that.

The light beam shifted as MacGregor began to move forward. Miranda responded without thinking. She aimed the rock she was holding and threw it with all her might. It found its mark: there was the crunch of glass breaking, and the torch flickered and went out, plunging the whole world into instant darkness.

Callum cursed under his breath, but Miranda had already disappeared, as surefooted as one of the moor ponies, not even a shadow in the murkiness where Callum was unable to even make out his hand as he held it before his face.

He worked his way gingerly back to where he had pulled the Magnette off the road, cursing the pride that had prompted him to cut the lights before going after the girl. *Didn't want the wrong eyes observing!* Now it took him long, precious moments to find the black, unmarked vehicle. Several times he scuffed and bruised his shins on unseen rocks and other obstructions. A fine mist of perspiration wet his forehead by the time he reached his destination and leaned, breathing heavily with relief, against the cool leather seat.

What to do now? It would be madness indeed to attempt to follow her; the moors were an untracked wilderness, and she could be heading anywhere—swallowed up by the land as she was. Even if he located someone who had a torch and would accompany him—someone who might guess better than he could—even then, they would be too late. The two would be well holed up against such an extremity.

He spread his arms over the steering wheel and rested his head for a moment. *Despondent.* That was the word for his mood. "Och, 'tis your pride, man," he muttered, "that you cannot win the girl's confidence." But he knew it was more than that. A sense of foreboding—a sixth sense grown from years of experience—made him fear for Miranda and the brother she so fiercely protected.

※

Miranda was tired and chilled when she reached the inn. Stephyn took her inside and insisted she drink something warm before heading out once more across the high moors to the hut where he had been concealing himself. It was a miserable place, offering little more than bare shelter. Miranda shivered as she sat down on a pile of hemp and old sacking, and hugged her arms to her while Stephyn lit a fire of peat and wood chips, scarcely large enough to heat them. She stretched her hands out to the flames.

"How long have you been here?" she asked.

"Several days. I arrived shortly after you returned."

"I thought you were going elsewhere—to some safe hiding place; that's what you told me."

"That's what I thought."

"What happened to change things?"

He ran his fingers through his thick dark hair and set the curls a tumble. "I can only tell you so much, Miranda, without placing you in the greatest of danger."

"You've already done that."

"I know . . . I know that!" His voice trembled and she shrank from meeting his eyes, so dark with misery.

"You have something that does not belong to you. That much I have figured out. *Give it back, Stephyn!* You are dealing with people who have no scruples, no feelings."

"It is not that simple!"

"It is that simple—look what happened to your friend, Jean."

Stephyn went pale and began to pluck nervously at a raveling end of the hemp upon which he sat. "I need something to bargain with."

"Why?"

"Because these men have used me for a guinea pig—trapped me."

"How, Stephyn . . . what do you mean?"

He let his breath out in a long, ragged sigh. "They have framed me, to make it look as though I have committed crimes that I had no part in; in this way they get people in their power. So when Jean suggested that we turn the game round on them, I agreed."

She shook her head slowly. "You are in over your head, Stephyn."

"No!" he demanded. "I ask for little in return. They can easily grant me what I wish without damaging their pride and power."

Miranda felt suddenly heavy, as though a terrible weight pinned her to the earth. "You should understand, Stephyn, if you've dealt with them at all, it is more than pride and power." She paused, struggling for words. "Call it expediency. It would simply not be wise to let you live after what you have done to them."

She could see by his expression that he did not believe her. "I must try it my way," he said. "I believe I can make it work, but I must have you out of Boscastle first."

She blinked back at him, uncomprehending. "What do you mean?"

"I don't want you here for them to harm, to use in any way. Could you manage to go stay with Bessie's sister in Penrith for a few days?"

"I don't know. What would I tell her?"

"Something—anything!" He was on a short fuse, she could see his emotions eating away at him, like a deadly acid. "Couldn't you arrange it?"

"I suppose so," she agreed woodenly. "But it will be neither easy nor pleasant. And, what about you?"

Briefly the thought ran through her head: *Tell him of Callum MacGregor. If he knows there is someone who might help him . . .*

Then she looked at his face, and remembered how he had acted in London. He would never throw himself upon the mercy of the inspector. It would only serve to frighten him further, impair his already faulty judgment.

"So when do you wish me to go, and for how long?" she asked, feeling petulant and unhappy. "It will arouse suspicions. People will think me crazy. I just returned from London—what do I say to Father and Bessie?"

He ignored her question entirely; in fact, she wondered if he even had heard her. "Leave at once . . . tomorrow . . . as soon in the day as possible."

She rose stiffly, her muscles aching a bit from the cold hard surface where she had sat so long without moving. "I'd best be going, Stephyn."

He rose to stand beside her, and she felt an awkwardness between them which was not usually there.

"When shall I hear from you?" she asked. "When will it be safe for me to return again?"

"I don't know, I can't say for certain."

"Stephyn! I won't endure this. I can't just be gone indefinitely, for no apparent reason. I shall come back in one week if I have not heard from you."

He knew she was cross with him. He lowered his eyes, by way of apology. "I'm so sorry, Miranda. What a muddle I've made of things. You've every right to despise me . . ."

"Hush!" she demanded. "Do not say such things, Stephyn. You know how well I love thee."

Of a sudden she placed her hands on his shoulders and gave him a kiss on the cheek. Then she turned and started out the low door into the clear, starlit night.

"I can find my way," she insisted, when he began to walk with her.

He said not a word, but took her cold hand in his, and they walked in silence—past the dark clusters of still, sleeping ponies, past the small noisy burn, past the clutter of black stones, sharp and jagged, until they reached a small green plain. Here, with reluctance, he stopped.

"I dare come no further."

She gave his hand a squeeze, then let it drop. "Go with God, Stephyn," she said under her breath, and watched as he turned and hurried in the other direction, head and body bent to his walking.

It grieved her to think of him returning to the cheerless, half-ruined cottage, cold and frightened and friendless. She spoke a little prayer in her heart for him, over and over again, as she crossed the last stretch of moors and descended to the quiet, sleeping village below.

Chapter Eight

The smell of the sea was strong in the air when Callum walked from the Harbour Light to the humped bridge over the Valency River. The air was gray and moist with a witch fog that hung like silt above him. The road sweeper was already out with his faded wheelbarrow, hunchbacked and gnarled like the cobbles he clattered across.

Pascal, the constable, was waiting for him, his face as gray as the morning. "They found another body at first light, a shepherd on the high moors discovered it. Thought you ought to know."

"Where?" Callum's voice came out creaky, and he cleared his throat.

"In one of the great tors, covered by rocks and brush."

Callum knew tor was the local name for one of the low dips that mark the country, usually beside streams or springs. "Has the body been identified?"

"Aye, I do fear 'tis one o' the local lads."

"Stephyn Symons."

The constable nodded. "Would you like to go out, sir, and see for yourself?"

Callum rode while Pascal drove his small, rather battered Morris by back roads Callum had no idea existed. He watched, fascinated, as they rose higher and higher before the car shuddered to a stop and the constable shut off the engine and pulled the brake.

"This be the end of the road; 'tis by foot the remainder of the way, I fear."

Callum was relieved to move his muscles, to feel the

chill air cool the hot skin of his face. He inwardly cursed the lad for his ignorance, Miranda for her stubbornness, and himself for his stupidity. The tor was a wide one, much filled in with the decaying mulch of leaves and rotting stumps. They had uncovered the body which lay as they had found it, with only the thin covering of tarpaulin to protect it from the glaring gaze of the living. Callum pulled back the canvas to reveal the boy's face.

He had never seen Stephyn at close quarters before. The features, though frozen in an expression of horror, were as finely drawn as a woman's: well-shaped, sensitive mouth, fine cheekbones and chin line, oval eyes set under a strong ledge of forehead, and thick, dark curls that were matted, like a child's hair who had been playing out in the wet.

"Have you a crowner—a coroner nearby?"

"Closest one is in Bude, nearly an hour away."

"We shall have to take him there. I want him carefully examined."

"As you say, gov'nor."

The two men were alone with the stiff, sightless boy, as though they stood on the very top of creation, where life no longer existed, only this endless, lifeless plain. Callum checked every inch of the ground, looking for footprints, fingerprints, anything unusual lost or dropped here.

"Cause of death?" he asked the constable, curious for his opinion.

"Well, he were beat up pretty bad p'rhaps a concussion."

"There is a very small, very tidy bullet hole at the base of his neck," Callum replied. "I suspect we shall find very little in the way of prints or evidence. These men were professionals, long on prudence as well as practice." Pascal was watching him respectfully. "Nevertheless, I'd like to make a wide circuit round this spot, see if we can discover tyre tracks, for instance. If I can link the make of auto with the Studebaker that was sighted here earlier, for instance . . ."

The constable was with him. Silently they parted, each going in a different direction, in ever-widening circles. Callum lost all awareness of time. The sun seemed to have forgotten to rise here; the air and earth were dank with an old, mouldy moisture that never thoroughly dried. Callum could taste it as he drew the scent in through his nostrils. At one point he stopped to remove his jacket, at another to drink greedily from a thin, bubbly spring.

At last he was rewarded. On a height where the grass and soil had worn thin to reveal the bare, shale-layered rock a very short cigarette butt, half-crushed by a heel mark, lay like a fragment of bleached bone. Callum slid a piece of paper beneath it and lifted it carefully up. Sure enough, not many yards off were the tyre marks he had hoped for, and evidence of a heavy object being dragged along the stony surface. Walking slowly over every inch they had covered, he suddenly let out a low cry. In a crevice of one of the jagged rocks was caught a piece, an infinitesimal piece, of tweed cloth; no more than a dozen threads, but such a fragment was more than ample.

Callum busied himself for another quarter of an hour before he stopped, stretched his muscles, and halloed for the constable, with the signal of two yelps followed by a long whistle. Soon the still air carried a faint repeating reply. He leaned against a great outcropping that looked like the prow of a ship, and waited. *I've one thing in my favor*, he thought. *These fellows are unaware of my presence. They believe they have only the locals to deal with, and thus little to fret themselves over. One little advantage that I must be careful to hold onto.*

He saw at some distance the Cornishman approaching and rose to meet him, anxious all at once to get going, to nail the cruel, nearly inhuman creatures who played so callously with other men's lives.

Callum sent the prints, the cloth fragment, and the cigarette butt to London by special messenger, a man named Nathan Reber who could be explicitly trusted. The body was removed. Callum wanted it not only carefully examined, but cleaned and made to look as presentable as possible before Miranda was allowed to look upon it. Miranda! He sent Pascal to handle the more mundane matters, and went in search of the young girl himself.

He found her at the inn shop waiting on a customer, so he ducked in and told Bessie Youlton, who swayed when she heard it, so that he had to steady her and help her to a nearby seat.

"You will 'ave your hands full with Miranda," she warned him. "I will say a prayer for the poor dear."

The shock was too great to allow her curiosity to surface, though Callum could recognize it lurking behind her eyes. What a mess this could turn into! He had told her only that the boy was found dead up on the high moors, but with all that had happened here lately, she could come to the conclusion of foul play with no prompting from him.

He returned to find Miranda free, straightening a shelf of colorful tea cozies. "Will you walk with me on the cliffs for a bit, lass?"

Her eyes held a wariness when she turned them upon him.

"I've already cleared it with Bessie," he said.

"Is it important?"

She spoke the words like a death knell, as though she sensed something.

"Aye, that it is."

Callum was afraid his eyes would betray him, but she came docily and moved with him down toward the harbor, then up the slope where they had walked together his first day here. The sky was still as gray as the sea below it. The sound of the water tearing at the patient rocks was so lonely!

She stopped when they reached the same lookout point and turned her sad eyes upon him. "What is it?" she said.

"It is the last thing you want to hear, Miranda. I pray God will lessen the blow for you—"

"Stephyn is dead." She put her hand to her mouth as she spoke the words. Then a cry came from her—a cry Callum would remember for the rest of his life.

She turned and fled from him, fleet and graceful as the red doe that live on the hills of Scotland. By the time he thought to move after her she was high above him, moving swiftly, nearly out of his vision. He took a few steps further, then stopped at the futility of it.

"Let her go, MacGregor," he growled under his breath. "Grant her at least the privacy of so terrible a grief."

He would go back and see how the official end of the matter was going. When Miranda reached the point where she was ready to talk to him, she would find him; he was certain of that.

*

She ran until her breath burned and the muscles in her tired legs trembled. She ran until she found herself on her knees, gulping large drafts of air, her head light and dizzy and her ears ringing. She did not know how long she crouched thus before she crawled into a stand of thick hawthorne bushes and began to weep uncontrollably. The force of her own grieving frightened her; she tried to check the choking sobs as they tore from her, but not until exhaustion claimed her was she able to stop the tears. Then she huddled with her knees hugged to her chin, occasionally moaning or wimpering like a child. The truth she had been so ferociously pushing from her settled like a dark clawed beast upon her chest and threatened to suffocate her.

He is dead because of you! the ugly voice taunted. *You left him helpless. You refused to tell him of the inspector—or to let*

MacGregor go with you. You could have saved him! You are senseless and stupid. You let him die!*

The accusation went round and round, like a white-hot iron, searing her heart, searing her senses with a deep, burning pain. Her strength was spent. She cowered before the onslaught of guilt and agony seeing only Stephyn's tortured face before her; hearing his voice, thin and frightened, begging forgiveness . . . begging mercy . . . begging one more chance to wrest his life back again.

༄

As he reached the narrow path at the foot of the cliffs Callum realized that there were other family members involved besides Miranda. He walked a few feet further where a view of the harbor opened up to him. He saw the round balding head of Morris May; it would be the decent thing to go down and tell the old man what had happened.

He took the steep slope slowly. Had the seaman, too, sensed something? He rose from his bench and approached the Scotsman, peering at him closely as he approached.

"There is that in yer eye that bodes ill, my friend," he observed, and his voice was still rich and deeply modulated; the voice of a much younger man.

"You speak but the truth, I fear," Callum responded. "I have sad tidings concerning your grandson, Stephyn."

Mr. May scowled, and the laugh lines in his broad face all ran together in an incongruous pattern. "He has been a troubled soul ever since returning from the war," he sighed. "What has befallen him now?"

"The last and worst. He was found in a tor on the moors last night, shot to death."

The old man squinted his eyes, as though at a blow. "Ahhh, I did hear the dogs last night set up such a howling and yelping."

Callum nodded. He knew what Morris May referred

to was often taken as a sign of impending death.

"So your sixth sense told you something?"

"We Celts, you should know, man, see through the thin veil separating this from the next world much better than most." He sighed and scratched at the growth on his chin. "His father be over yonder. Will ye come wi' me?"

"Of course I will."

Wilford Symons did not look up from his work until the two men stood before him and Callum cleared his throat meaningfully.

"What be it?" he growled as he straightened his large, muscled frame and trained his cold eye on them.

" 'Tis a proper shame ye have forgotten yer manners, Will," his father-in-law scolded. "Mr. Forsyth has come here on our behalf."

When Symons did not respond, Callum said briefly, but kindly, "Your son was found dead on the moors late last night, sir. I am sorry, indeed, to have to bring you such news."

The dull eyes seemed to glaze over. Callum saw his cheek muscles twitch, but there was no other visible sign.

"So much the better," the man muttered at length. "It be as it should be."

Callum's eyes widened in question, but the grandfather shook his white head and motioned him to silence.

"Well, my sincere condolences to you both." Callum touched the diced green balmoral he wore in brief respect, then turned on his heel and walked up the banked curve of the old pier without once turning round. He was musing upon the singular reaction of the dead boy's father, and storing it carefully in the catalog of his mind, in the event he might have further use of it in the dark days to come.

༃

They had brought him to the church, he already lay

there, with only the dim candles to light him, waiting for her.

Miranda had wandered, stunned and aimless, for what must have been hours. If she stopped, if she held still, the thoughts and feelings rushed in again, and they were too much to bear. When she had worn herself out to the point of utter exhaustion, she stumbled back to her house, curled up in a little ball on her bed and slept.

When she awoke, it was dark, both outside her window and inside her closed room. She knew at once that the house was empty, save for herself. Her father must surely have been told by this time, and her grandfather. She could not help feeling a great relief that her father was not here. He would withdraw even further into himself; she was well acquainted with the effect of grief upon him.

She arose slowly, as though movement of all sorts was painful, as though her very body was cumbersome to the thin, intangible substance of her soul. She washed her face in cold water and patted it dry. Then she changed into a gray dress made of soft wool, the closest thing to black that she owned. She brushed her long hair back and twisted it into a knot at her neck, securing it with the pale ivory combs her mother had given her. Then she walked very slowly down the silent street toward the church which huddled like a shadow over the shadowed graveyard.

She had no idea what the time was, nor did she think of it. She drew a breath as delicate and trembly as the beating of a moth's wings as she pushed open the thick wooden door and slipped into the interior where even the dim lights made her eyes blink and squint to adjust.

She walked down the long aisle deliberately, almost reluctantly. Callum watched her, half-convinced she was an other-worldly figure come to welcome the dead. Her thin, long fingers were clasped in front of her, like the white folded wings of a bird. She did not pause until they rested over the coffin, like two lifeless hands clasped in prayer. She stood a long time looking down, her face revealing nothing of what she was feeling inside. Then her body curved in one smooth graceful motion and she placed her long cold fingers on the frozen brow, then wove them through the thick locks of dark hair.

"Who brought him here?"

Callum started with surprise, realizing her first words were addressed to him. He was not even certain she had observed him there in the shadows.

"Raymond Pascal and myself. We were most careful of him."

Only her eyes blinked in acknowledgment. "My father?"

"I told both your father and your grandfather myself."

"Thank you for that." Her voice was toneless, yet light and airy like a seraph's voice, promising pure, unspoken things. "Has my father been here?"

Callum hesitated only momentarily. "He has not yet seen Stephyn, no." When she made no response, he added, "Your grandfather came, his white hair round his round face like an angel's. He sang to the lad, some low, mournful sea lay."

She nodded then, and closed her eyes, as though she could picture the details of the scene to herself. "That is well," she said.

They lapsed into a silence that grew so long, so strained that Callum could hear the rise and fall of his own breathing. At last her voice came again, small as a sigh in the great, hollow place.

"Did he suffer much?"

Callum winced at the question, but her eyes were searching his face. "I believe he did. But death, when it came, was swift and merciful."

"More merciful than I," she said. "For, in truth, it is I who killed him."

Callum looked at her carefully, not trying to dissemble. "It is not so."

She stared back at him, wide-eyed and childlike. "Did I not refuse to allow you to accompany me, then make it impossible for you to follow? Did I not hesitate, and then choose wrongly in not telling him of you? I left him friendless, with no recourse—entirely at the mercy of evil."

Her calm, deliberate words disarmed Callum. Why this scathing self-recrimination? "You speak from your heart, not your head."

"I speak truth."

"He had his agency, Miranda, and his enemies were determined; one time or another, they would have had their way."

"If he were in your custody, if he were under protection?"

"Very likely, even then."

Her eyes burned with an unexpressed accusation; she did not in the least whit believe him.

"Your self reproach is colored by self-pity. That would not please your brother," Callum ventured, but his voice was very tender as he spoke the harsh words.

"You know how to wound," she replied, "you who knew Stephyn not at all."

She suddenly lifted her head in that characteristic way of hers, like a doe testing the wind. "There is no wake. Is the wake to be tomorrow?"

"There is to be no wake; so your father decreed it."

"That right is not his," she hissed. "May heaven have mercy upon him."

Deil take it, Callum thought, *these Symonses are a strange lot!*

Miranda moved, with that same unhurried, unconscious elegance which was so disarming, and lowered herself to sit on a low stool at the head of the coffin. "I will stay with him," she announced. "I will not leave him here—at the end he will no longer be all alone."

"Then I will stay with you," Callum replied, and at once moved back where the soft shadows half hid his face.

She did not object; her eyes said she felt his sympathy and accepted it. He leaned back against the hard wall and closed his eyes. But all sorts of dark, half-formed images played across the blind surface, so he opened them again and gazed at the shimmery, shadowy figure of the young girl, all gray and golden, who sat with such solemn patience in the presence of death.

Chapter Nine

The golden rays of the sun spreading like flaming arrows to pierce the horizon of the sea had faded, and a dirty, gusty wind had blown up, drawing a yellow fog from the wet earth which the rain had saturated hours before. Callum was sorry to see it. He blew on his fingers and searched in his pockets for his mittens. This burial would be a dismal enough affair without the elements contriving against them as well.

The service in the dark stone church had been almost eerie, the minister speaking of the dead man in very intimate terms: recalling his childhood, his deep and sensitive nature, his service to his country; and saying strange things such as, "The noble lad has already been snatched from the grasping fingers of death; now that shadow has closed upon him, and he is free from the darkness and trials of the flesh."

Callum had never observed the melancholy nature of the Cornish people up close before. It disarmed him a little as he looked out over the somber faces of neighbors and countrymen filling the narrow, close pews. He suspected that a number were there out of curiosity, for the talk had surely gone round. A murdered Frenchman, a stranger, was one matter, but a lad of their own? That was lamentable indeed.

Burial at night. He had heard seamen ofttimes prefer this, yet he believed this was Wilfred's doing: no wake to honor a son who had disgraced himself, burial by stealth, when the sun would not be forced to look down on their work.

Fog hung from the black tree branches like witches'

tatters and rose from humped mounds where those long dead already slumbered. Callum, walking with the solemn procession, felt the hairs at the back of his neck rise. He sensed the presence of things otherworldly, and he was not such a man.

While they lowered Stephyn's casket into the gaping hole that awaited it some women near the back began a high, chanting wail that shivered over the air and twisted itself into the keen of the vexing wind. Miranda was ahead of him, he could not see her features, could not tell how she was doing. She stood still and serene, like a statue of one of the three graces, somehow beyond all that is mortal, yet Callum knew better than that. After a prayer, and a hymn that was terribly dirgelike, the mourners began to drift away, fading into the thickening fog like so many apparitions.

Callum stood to one side and watched the narrow paths empty and silence re-claim its own. Four people remained at the graveside—and he realized for the first time that the young man who was a stranger to him had his arm cupped protectively beneath Miranda's right elbow. He rocked back on his heels and studied the stranger for a moment: he was tall and as slender as a sapling the wind has not bent. He had a prominent brow, and a quiet way about him; that was the most Callum could tell from his distance. He began to inch forward a bit.

Just then the old man turned and planted a kiss on his granddaughter's cheek. "I'm off to me bed, dearie. Don't you stay in this sad place too long, my dear."

Wilfred Symons glowered from under a scowling brow. "I be on my way, too. 'Tis done at last; the lad is where he should have been years ago."

Miranda turned on him, her fingers clawing her companion's arm. "How can you speak of him so? Have ye no heart whatsoever? Would you have denied him *life*—the sweetness of the sea at morning, the cries of the birds, the pure air in his lungs? Would you have denied *her* the saving of him? Did you despise her, too?"

Her father answered her slowly, and his words, when he spoke, had no ring to them, no life at all. "I loved her! And I was fool enough to let her love me—and waste her young life for my sake and his."

Why did the dull words cut through him like ice? Callum shivered and touched his hat to the two men as they walked past.

"Say the lines for me, will you, Francis? . . . Say them for Stephyn."

The tall man stood a little straighter and began in a voice as deep and quiet as Miranda's, as rich with controlled emotion.

"They shall not grow old, as we that are left to grow old . . ."

Callum recognized the words at once. They were part of the most popular poem of the Great War, and were nearly always quoted at soldiers' graves, or annually at ceremonies held before the new war memorials every small community had built to honor their dead.

"Age shall not weary them, nor the years condemn . . . At the going down of the sun and in the morning, we shall remember them . . ."

Miranda listened dry-eyed. Then she said simply, "Leave me now, Francis, please."

The lad did as he was bid and walked past Callum without glancing at him. The moon, obscured by the fog, throbbed wierdly, its light nothing but a shadow behind the gray mist. Callum heard a low moan, as though the sea were complaining within its vast shores. Then he saw Miranda lift her head and freeze, listening, watching, and the realization seeped into him that one could not hear the moan of the sea from here.

When the sound repeated itself, he felt a cold prickle lift all the hairs of his back. The white shape; dull, yet somehow glowing, drifting and insubstantial, appeared for the blink of an eye, then was gone. But Miranda dropped to her knees beside one of the gravestones, and cried out piteously, "Mother, please, do not grieve; do not torment yourself!"

Callum rubbed at his eyes, then, fascinated, took a few steps forward, closer to where the girl was kneeling—looking up pleadingly into the face of another woman, nearly as young and comely as herself, yet with a radiance about her person.

"I am sorry I failed you, Mother." Miranda was weeping now. When Callum glanced again nothing was there save the shadows, and the trailing gray branches that waved in the wind.

Callum went to her side and lifted her up very gently. "I will take you home now," he said, and she did not object. They walked over the carpet of leaves and moss, spongy beneath their feet, to where his black car sat waiting. He handed her into the passenger's side and tucked a plaid blanket around her knees. The engine humming into life was one of the homeliest sounds Callum had ever heard.

They drove in silence up the steep curved streets to the narrow row of seamen's cottages, glowing white even in the fog, their slate roofs glistening beneath the clouds of moisture which half-obscured them. Hard as the rock of the hillside they were, untouched by wind or weather; put in place nearly six hundred years ago and meant to endure long after this frail girl and her heartaches had become dim memories, and less—only vague whispers upon the sea wind.

"I'll stay as long as you'd like," Callum said. "Is your father within?"

"Down at the pub until the wee hours when they chase him out. Then, like as not, he'll sleep on his boat. He's more comfortable there."

Callum could not bear it. Her eyes were so terrible. He opened the door and pushed her gently inside. "You take off your damp things while I make some tea," he instructed.

She complied in this new, docile manner of hers. He set the kettle on to boil, easily locating the few things he needed: spoons, cups, a bowl of sugar cubes, and some strong herbal concoction he found that looked as though it might do the trick. Miranda came out in a thick robe, looking thoroughly benumbed and exhausted. He made her sit down and sip the hot liquid nearly gone before he led her to the small back room which he knew was hers, because it looked and smelled like her. He tucked her in as he would a small child, crooning bits of old Scottish tunes without knowing it. The saddest of smiles touched the ends of her mouth.

"I will be here," he told her. "Sleep, lass. Sleep, if you can."

He sat himself down in the parlor; clean, but cheerless in comparison to Miranda's sanctuary. He lit an oil lamp, set his own mug of tea on the table beside him, and prepared for his vigil.

꒳

He must have dozed a little. He woke with the strongest impression that someone else was in the room. He lifted his eyelids slowly, and at first saw nothing that had not been there before.

"Sorry I woke you, but I had to know for myself that Miranda is safe."

Callum blinked at the tall, slender figure whose blue eyes looked back at him, gentle and patient. He was very young, but the smooth skin of his face was already creased with "sea lines," especially about his deep eyes.

"You were with Miranda," Callum said, "but I've not seen you around these parts before."

His visitor laughed, quietly, as though he was keenly aware of the exhausted girl sleeping in the next room. "I be Boscastle born 'n bred; you're the stranger here, man!"

Callum's mouth twisted in a lopsided response. "You've the right of it. But where have you been, that you show up of a sudden this way?"

"Shippin' off me uncle's vessel down at Newquay. When I heard what happened to Stephyn, I headed back as fast as I could."

Callum nodded.

"And what brings you to perform this very personal service for Miranda?" the youth demanded.

"I've got myself in the habit of looking after her; no one else seems to."

The boy looked askance and Callum set his jaw. "That's the best you'll get right now; you'd best settle for it. Francis, is it?"

"Francis Callaway."

"Rory Forsyth," Callum responded, sticking out his hand, surprised at the size and the sinewy strength of the long, thin fingers as they closed over his own. "Have a cup of tea, man," he offered. Francis poured himself a large mug, grabbed the tin of biscuits and came in to sit opposite Callum.

"What is it with this family?" Callum asked. "Why is Wilfred Symons so hard and bitter, so calloused to life?"

Francis hesitated.

"I've more right than you know to the information," Callum growled. "Talk to me, man!"

"There be a story, a very long one."

Callum spread his hands out. "I have all night."

Francis shrugged his shoulders and rubbed at his chin. "I don't rightly know where to start."

"Back. Back as far as you know."

"All right, then. When Wilfred Symons was a young man he married Florence, the oldest of the May girls, sister to Miranda's mother."

Even that explained some things. "Go on," Callum said, trying not to appear too eager.

"They were well-suited, and happy together. She brought out in him things you would not dream of, seeing him now. When he learned that she carried his baby, it seemed their happiness was complete. He fussed over her as scarce befits a rough seaman, but when it came time for the fishing, his place was out with the boats. That autumn was a wild one. The fleet met with a storm and were marooned on a small island for several days before they could make their way home. The storm, the old wives say, brought the child's birth on early, and there were complications no one could have anticipated—"

"And Florence died."

"That's right. Only weeks after giving birth to the infant. 'Twere that terrible, the old ones tell it—they tried to wait for the fishermen, but in the end they had to bury her before her husband came back."

"Merciful heaven," Callum murmured.

"Aye, 'twas near beyond bearing. When Wilfred found out what had happened he was all for tearing her grave apart to hold her once more in his arms. 'Twas a pity to see him, they say, mad with pain as he was."

"And the child? Stephyn, I assume."

"Yes, Stephyn. The girl's mother took him, and all her sisters fussed over him—the young one especially. Lena they called her, and she was only fourteen when her sister died."

After Miranda, Callum could picture her easily.

" 'Twere a harsh winter, that one. The baby was pale and sickly, despite all the attention lavished upon him. Wilfred could not bear the sight of him; it brought *her* too much to mind. He took to the sea whenever the chance was given, taking risks such as no seaman had a mind to share with him—unmindful of anything, save the pain that ate him inside."

Francis drained his cup and rose to pour fresh, hot liquid. "The child contracted whooping cough that winter and, after that, he just seemed to waste away. The old doctor grew solemn and began to shake his head at the anxious women. Long about February, when Wilfred came in to port, his mates told him he'd best go set eyes on his son before they buried him, too.

"He burst into the house wild-eyed, and none but the young one could calm him, placing the boy in his arms, crooning over the both of them. But there was no peace for him. He left and walked the cold shoreline until his teeth were rattling in his head, and then she came to him; down where the breakers were boiling—Florence rose up right out of the sea."

Callum had seen and experienced many things in his years on the Force, but nothing of this nature that was so real, so gripping.

"To his utter astonishment, she told him she was shamed at the way he neglected their child, and she was taking him to herself. 'You will marry again,' she told him, 'and forget me. But Stephyn is mine.'

"He was beside himself, begging for mercy, but she would have none of it. In torment he stumbled back to her family and told them the tale. Her father turned pale and her mother wept, but the youngest daughter crept out into the wild night and sought the same lonely stretch of sea. There, battered by wind and spray, she held her arms out and pled for the life of the child. 'I will raise him myself,' she promised her dead sister. 'I will care for him, and I will care for Wilfred, who is near demented without you.' "

Callum could picture it; he could picture it all too vividly.

"No one knows what Lena saw or heard there. But when she returned, soaked to the skin and shivering, there was a calmness about her that no one quite understood. The next morning the child was noticeably improved, and each day he grew stronger and rosier." Francis glanced up at the stranger who was listening attentively, his deep eyes sympathetic and warm. "Less than a year later, when she was yet fifteen, Lena became Wilfred's wife."

"Was it her I saw?" Callum wondered aloud. "In the cemetery with Miranda?"

"You saw—"

"I saw something that was more than a vague apparition—it was a woman, full formed. Miranda spoke to her; in fact, she called her Mother."

Callum's revelation plainly distressed the younger man. "Did their meeting seem to upset Miranda?"

"I canna say for certain. She knelt by the headstone and begged forgiveness; I can tell you that much."

There was a moment of heavy silence. "Why does she feel so responsible for this brother—as though the angels, themselves, had given her charge of him?"

Francis grimaced, and the lines in his face cut deeper. "You've very near named it, my man. When her mother died, right after the war had ended, Miranda was but a child of ten years. 'You are nearly as old as I when I began taking care of him,' she told her daughter. 'You must take over now, you must keep him from harm. Florence and I will watch over you, but the task will be yours.' "

Callum shuddered visibly, rose and paced the room, greatly agitated. "Too much," he muttered, "too much for such a wee lass." He felt an anger against these two women who had manipulated the living beyond their right. Heaven help her, what she must have been through!

Francis watched him, curious himself about the things this stranger had not yet told him. "We have much talking left, we two," he said finally.

"Indeed, you are right," Callum responded, for he had made some decisions of his own while the young man spun his tale. "Are you in love with her?"

Unoffended, Francis answered forthrightly. "I have been since I knew what the word meant."

"And Miranda?"

"She cares well for me; but Stephyn has always stood squarely between us. She could see very little during these last troubled years, beyond her duty to him."

"You have your chance now to stand between her and her misery—to stand between her and danger."

Francis leaned forward.

"Too late to tell you now; my old eyes are drooping with weariness."

"Tomorrow?"

"Aye, tomorrow first thing."

Francis settled back against the support of his chair. "Mind if I stay with you?"

"I'd like that," Callum said.

"I know the cupboard where the extra blankets are kept. We can make ourselves comfortable enough."

Callum was not sure about that. Police work did not usually dig so deep into the souls of the lives it touched. All his hard-won callouses were softening in the Cornish sea air. He felt ill equipped for the job he was doing right now. And this compassion, that singed like a flame, made a poor bedfellow, indeed.

Chapter Ten

Miranda slept through the night. When the morning found its way through the narrow, deeply set windows of the old cottage and Callum awoke, he discovered that both she and Francis had gone, leaving him a note on the kitchen table.

Have gone for breakfast at the inn and some fresh air, Francis had written. Then, hastily scribbled beneath the words, he had added: *Will stand as you asked me to.*

Callum remembered telling the boy: *This is your chance to stand between her and danger.* He felt a sense of relief that was exhilarating. After a quick wash and a couple of last night's biscuits, he drove to the Harbour Light and asked Bessie if he might use their private phone.

"'Twere right decent of you to watch over the girl last night."

Callum rubbed his fingers through his unruly hair. "Who in the world told you that?"

She smiled smugly. "Folk have their ways here."

He patted her hand, and the warm gesture gave her courage to ask, "Are we all in danger, sir, do you think?"

"No," Callum replied. "As long as you are careful—a bit more than usual."

"But Miranda?"

"Miranda is in danger," he said.

"We can get her out of here!" Bessie clawed at his arm. "I've a sister in Bude who would be happy for the company of—"

"Bessie," Callum soothed. "Between Francis and myself

". . . we'll take care of her. Perhaps, in time, your plan will prove to be the best one."

She was both confused and curious as she watched Mr. Forsyth pass through the inner door into their private parlor, but the ordinary demands of the day nursed her away from her dangerous preoccupation with what the professor had said.

Callum rang the Yard, using the commissioner's private extension. As he reported all that had happened, he could almost see the little man leaning forward and scratching at his bare head eagerly.

"MacGregor, your lad may have been framed as you believe, but the record shows him mixed up in half a dozen nasty affairs."

"I'd like to clear his name when we clear this whole mess up."

"That might be possible. We have the lab report back. The cigarette was a Camel, one of the strongest American brands."

"American car, American smokes," Callum mused. "The cloth fragment?"

"From a tweed jacket made in the Scottish Highlands and popular in London just now."

Callum chuckled.

"But it is of a costly make, they assure me. And you'll be pleased to hear this. The impression you sent of the tyre tread matches the very Studebaker make you described seeing in Boscastle."

Callum was elated. For the first time some of the necessary pieces were falling in place.

"You think they killed the lad because he wouldn't tell them where the goods were stashed?"

"No." Callum was thoughtful. "I believe, after roughing him up a bit, they promised him his life if he'd tell. He didn't believe them, so he told the wrong location. I'd bet on it, Thomas."

"One of your hunches, eh? What in the world has he got in there?"

"More than we believe, or something altogether different from what we've yet thought of. I think he was protecting someone—or something—very, very important, and hoping to strike a deal that would clear his name and assure him protection as well."

"The boy was a fool."

"Aye," Callum agreed, the syllable ending in a long sigh. "I have the coast guard and some of the local fishermen watching for any strange vessels plying these shorelines."

"They'll be mad as wet hornets when they don't find what they're looking for."

"Then they'll come after the sister," Callum said, through clenched teeth.

"I'd best send you another man or two, MacGregor."

"We're nowhere near a showdown yet," Callum protested.

"You don't know that, man!"

"I know that another stranger in these parts will stick out like a sore thumb and stir things up to the point that even the 'bad guys' will grow suspicious, and that could well blow everything." He paused. "Anyway, I've found myself a mate of me own."

"Oh, you have?"

Callum told Thomas Howe all about Francis Callaway, not overly stating his qualifications, less his superior suspect manipulation. After listening carefully—a rare quality, and one of the commissioner's strong points—he gave his cautious approval to the plan. "If this fisherman doesn't work out, you won't let your pride get in the way, will you, MacGregor? You'll admit you were wrong, and come get the help you need."

"You've my word," Callum assured him. "There is too much at stake."

When he rang off he called the constable's number in

Tintagel and asked Pascal to meet him at the Harbour Light that afternoon. Then he checked in the gift shop, relieved to find Miranda there at her post.

"Sure you're up to this?" he asked her.

"'Tis much easier than sitting at home alone, or wandering the hills brooding."

Callum nodded.

"Thank you for staying last night."

Callum couldn't be sure, but he thought she colored a little when thanking him. The soft hue became her.

"You're welcome," he told her, unable to say all the other things in his mind.

"Do you have any idea where Francis went?"

She looked at him oddly. "He said to tell you he'd be at the Napoleon, waiting for you."

"Very good." Callum was pleased. "You take care now," he cautioned her; she looked back at him with that same puzzled air.

As he turned to walk away she called after him, using his real name without thinking. "Mr. MacGregor, you saw her, didn't you?"

Callum turned around slowly. The shop was empty, save for the two of them. "I saw her, Miranda, moving through the trees, standing behind the gravestone. She was nearly as lovely as you."

Her eyes misted over, and she could not manage the smile she attempted. Callum caught her hand up and pressed his lips against it. "Would to heaven I could spare you this suffering, lass," he murmured. "Let go a little, Miranda, lest you die of the pain."

He left her watching after him, and walked the distance to the Napoleon at the other end of the road. The main street of Boscastle boasted a large stable and a warehouse at the harbor end, Webber's Garage, a mill, a carpenter's shop, a doctor's surgery, as well as the two inns, a few odd shops, and a couple of pubs thrown in. Callum couldn't believe how he had come to enjoy being here, even under the present circumstances. The place was well-aged; it looked like something left over from a bygone era, preserving the mystique of both the land and the sea which had kept it alive. Even the people themselves, largely unaware of change and progress, seemed in touch with the basic, vital elements of life, undisturbed by frivolities which had distracted the masses of society during the Twenties. Something deep and elemental within himself felt at peace in this place; and for an errant moment he truly wished he were an ailing professor, free to dig into the very roots of Cornwall and make his own place here.

Francis was attentive. He listened carefully to Callum's lengthy explanation of all that had happened since he first called on Miranda in London. When a thing particularly disturbed him he would make a little clicking sound in the back of his throat, and tighten the muscles of his lean face, so that the bones stood in relief and the lines etched there hardened, and he looked as formidable an enemy as Callum would want to meet.

"Surely we can find something to give us an excuse to confront these devils and put them under lock and key."

"The law does not work that way. They are canny, and they have clever, unprincipled advocates, who wouldn't let us get near them. And then, you see, they would be on to us, and what advantage we have would be gone."

"What must we do then?" Francis's voice was deadly quiet.

"'Catch them in the act,' as the phrase goes."

"Murdering someone?"

Callum smiled grimly. "That would do. If we knew where this wretched hiding place was, we could 'innocently' lead them to it, and catch them with the loot red-handed. We must bide our time until we feel the prime moment come . . . and be prepared to pounce all at once."

"What of the tyre tracks, and the positive evidence you've acquired?"

Callum nodded. "We could take them in on that, and perhaps even hold one or two of them, but they would simply send more."

"But perhaps they would not kill again with such abandon."

"That is a possibility." Callum leaned closer, lowering his voice. "If we can just catch them prowling the waters, Pascal can take them in for questioning—with you and I no obvious part of it. They would expect the locals to be up in arms, finding one of their own brutally murdered. We might get away with holding onto the 'fall guy,' the least important of them, and at least putting him out of commission."

"That sounds reasonable," Francis said, relaxing a little.

"Ah, but one must follow it through. The powers that be are already sick of this matter, irritated to the point of incaution. This would anger them more. They could do anything, even start killing innocent citizens one by one, until the horrified community agreed to do for them what they could not do for themselves."

"Namely—?"

"Take to their boats en masse, comb the cliffs and coves, search every inch of the shoreline until Stephyn's hiding place was uncovered."

Francis's face darkened. "Yes, I see. You're right. I hadn't thought of all that."

"It does get your ire up, lad. Go ahead and fume a bit."

Callum rose, patting the younger man on the shoulder. "Your priority at all times is Miranda." His face broke into a slow smile. "But then, of course, you know that."

༜

He left Francis sitting in the pub and returned to the Harbour Light, where Raymond Pascal was waiting.

"Had a report just before I left my office," he said, as Callum entered. "A couple of fishermen out by Meachard

Island, not far from Boscastle harbor, sighted a large motorboat with three men in 'er."

Callum perked up at once. "Did they hail her?"

"That they did, sir, but she headed away from them, full speed. Never got within shouting distance of her again."

"I'll be!" Callum pounded his fist on the table. "Were they close enough to get any description?"

"Said they were definitely not locals; wore spanking new clothes—natty sailing duds, not the working garb and gear of the seaman."

"Anything else?"

"I read them the descriptions you left me, but the men hunched over soon as they saw they were spotted. The fishermen wanted to help, but 'twould only be guessing, at best, I fear."

"Of course. Well, at least we've alerted them to the idea that someone may be watching them."

"Is that good or bad, sir?"

"A little of both. Could mean they'll lay low for a while, or choose early morning and late evening to do their exploring. Better double our watch at that time, as far up and down the coast from this point as we're able."

Pascal nodded. "You 'ave it, sir."

"I'm to be notified if something happens—if the slightest thing happens—no matter how late the hour."

"Understood, sir. What about Frank and Bessie, if I should happen to come waking you at three o'clock of the morning?"

"They must be kept in the dark as long as possible—I must still be Rory Forsyth to them. I have a key to the back door; I'll copy it for you. Then you can slip up to the third floor, where my room is, probably without being heard."

Raymond Pascal scowled a little; this brand of police work was a bit beyond him.

"If worse comes to worse, simply tell them you've deputized me—give them a line; you know, 'he's a bright fellow, level-headed, and he has nothing else to do with his time.'"

Pascal liked that explanation. "We'll get things to rights," he assured Callum.

"Remember," Callum warned him. "Francis Callaway is as much undercover as I am. But you can contact him if for any reason you can't find me. In fact, inform him whenever you can do so discreetly, of what's going on. And Miranda Symons . . . keep a watchful eye out for her."

"Top priority, be she?"

"That's right."

He had nearly said, "It would mean a lot to me if you did." He guessed it was all right to care what happened to this girl. He had never had his own daughter, never had the chance with Annie dying so young. He guessed it was all right if he didn't let it impair his judgment. Little good he would do her if sloppiness on his part got her into more danger than she was already in.

He walked out with the constable. The thin clouds of the morning had thickened into a ceiling of steel gray, streaked through with great moving swirls of black.

"Sou'wester building," Pascal observed. "Could be real nasty by evening."

"Just what we need," Callum growled. "I'd like to get on with this business. Waiting out Mother Nature is something I'm not much accustomed to. If our friends have to lay low for too long, they'll get restless—"

"Mebbe make a mistake or two."

Callum grinned at the bristly Cornishman. "Yes, maybe they will."

"Let's you and I hope for it, leastways. There be no harm in hoping, you know."

Callum parted ways with Pascal and headed down to the harbor, where he hoped to find Wilfred Symons. As Stephyn's father he could be in some danger, too. Though Callum wondered if that would mean anything to the taciturn man who was too far beyond feeling to give comfort to the suffering girl who was so much in need of his care.

Chapter Eleven

Callum did not find Wilfred Symons down by the inner pier, but the old grandfather was there giving the hull of his ship a new coat of paint.

"How fare you?" Callum asked.

"Ah, I be like this boat here, battered and broken, paint cracked by the sun, but still willing to ride out each new wave as she comes to me."

"Well." Callum knew not what to say to the merry-faced man, who showed no sign of his grief, save a certain sadness in eyes that normally sparkled and danced.

"You think me uncaring, but I knew my grandson better than most did. He was not well suited to this life; some aren't, you know. He'll be happier in that place where he's gone."

So matter-of-fact, Callum thought. *The Celtic certainty of a life after this.* "What of his father?"

"That be a different story. That one courts his own misery, and then nurses it well."

"Do you not resent him, man, for how he used your daughters?"

Morris May paused in his work and looked hard at the stranger. "That be none of your business. But, seeing as I like you, professor, I'll tell you this much. It be not my place to judge any man living, least of all him who my girls chose to love."

Callum bit his tongue. For he wished to reply, "Aye, but was either of them truly happy with him?"

The old man, watching him, chuckled. "You be too

young, Mr. Forsyth, to understand. The ideal you college men talk about, it doesn't exist, no matter how much you try to hang onto it."

"Some live further from the ideal than others," Callum persisted.

Morris chuckled again. "You intellectual men love to argue for the very sake of it, don't you?" But he, too, was enjoying himself. "Aye, you speak rightly. But there be others who live in tune with the finest things of life and don't even know it, because it's so natural to them."

"Those are the genuine ones," Callum said softly, "who make a real difference, no matter where they may be living, or what they may do."

"Shame on ye, man!" There was a note to the old man's voice Callum had not before heard there. "Every man's life be a wonder in itself; every man's life makes a difference and goes on far beyond himself; you ought to be mindful of that."

I ought to be, Callum thought, duly subdued. *I know so little, my own life has been so narrow. Who am I to spout off?*

He shook the strong, gnarled hand Morris May offered him, and went on his way with the uncomfortable feeling that he possessed far fewer answers than he had thought he did, and that there were questions, many magnificent questions, he was totally ignorant of.

༣

As night settled over the gray, slate-roofed buildings of Boscastle and descended to meet the gray sea, the wind became raw, spitting a brittle rain, like the scattering of sharp pebbles, from the muddy expanse of the sky. At the Napoleon the lamps shone thickly and the steam from hot pasties and bacon and potato pies rose with tantalizing aromas against the low-hanging rafters, smoke-blackened from generations of constant use.

Wilfred Symons sat at one of the bar stools warming his hands around a mug of hot mahogany, picking now and again at the plate of pilchards that rested before him.

"Toss me a few more 'fair maids' from that hot batch," he called to the waiter.

"'Fair maids?'" inquired the stranger who came up and sat beside him.

Wilfred glowered, his eyes veiled as he examined the man whose dark blond hair was cropped fashionably short and whose finely etched mouth had a cruel curve to it. "That be our name for the fish"—he indicated his plate—"these little pilchards, that's all."

The smirk on the stranger's face did not go unnoticed. Wilford seemed to rouse himself, sit straighter in his seat, so that the bulk and size of him were visible. "Give this fellow here half a dozen 'fair ladies,'" he called out. "On me."

The stranger was visibly surprised, and eyed him a little more closely. "Gordon Willis," he said, "from London."

"Strange accent for London," Wilfred barked.

"Actually, I've lived all over: Antwerp, Paris, New York—"

The Cornishman snorted, to assure his companion that he was not impressed. "Then what brings you to this godforsaken corner of England?"

"Land," Willis answered at once. "Land here still goes for nothing; yet, mark my words, it will be dear as London property one day."

"Dear by whose standards?"

The gentleman shrugged, not finding it necessary to explain himself further to this man.

Wilfred called for another drink, a stronger one this time. After downing a generous portion and smacking his lips, he turned again to his companion. "'Ave a son, me only son. He was shot and killed three days ago."

The stranger's face registered surprise, and his eyes narrowed cautiously. "I am sorry to hear that," he replied, his voice even and careful. "How did it happen?"

"Ah, he was a bad lot in some ways, was Stephyn," Wilfred mumbled. "'Twere no accident, that much is for certain."

The stranger sat tense and listening. Wilfred finished off the rest of his drink and called for another, then leaned in close to the city man. "I b'lieve he were mixed up in something, I do."

The stranger smiled thinly. "You mean, he brought it on himself, in a manner of speaking?"

The big hand of the Cornishman clenched into a fist, but he answered in the same offhand manner. "'Spose there be at least some truth to that statement."

Those men sitting close by began to take note of the conversation. Their disapproval showed in their tightened brows. One or two shook their heads gravely.

"The worst of it is," Wilfred continued, "that the lad's left me high and dry. No one to help support me, not now, not in me old age. This rheumatism bites deep." He shook his own head and hunched over the stool again. "In five years, six years, I might not be able to fish at all."

"Now, Will—" one of his mates said, leaning over to pat him reassuringly on the back.

"Don't you 'now, Will' me, Ginger!" Wilfred growled. "You will 'ave your three strappin' lads to look after ye, an' each one true blue—*to be trusted.*"

He spoke the last words with emphasis, and Ginger Fry glowered back at him. "You best put that drink down now, Will, and head on back home."

Wilfred Symons ignored him and called out his request for another, but the bartender shook his head. "Go fill your skull with a little fresh air, Will," he said, "an' then you can come back for more."

Wilfred rose unsteadily, stood at his full height and gazed around him with a blank expression. "'Tis a cryin' shame, that's what it is," he called out in a loud voice, "that I be reduced to this, an' not one of you smug blokes 'ere bearin' an ounce of pity for me."

He stumbled for the door, and the men let him go, exchanging glances with one another before they settled once more to their meals and their drinks. No one seemed to notice that the strange gentleman paid his bill with dispatch and left the pub hastily, looking neither to left nor to right.

༄

There had been no sound to break the stillness; Callum had thought he would surely hear the constable if he came up the back stairs. And why this hand over his mouth, shutting his breath off?

He sat up and stretched to reach the lamp on the bedside table. As the black room leapt into light he nearly froze with astonishment. The man bent over him was half again as large as Raymond Pascal, his muscled face lean and well-lined, his straight brown hair laced with gray. He removed his hand and took a step or two backward.

"You will 'ave to pardon my methods, man," he said in a low monotone. "I surely did not wish to alert the house."

Callum stared at Wilfred Symons. "What are you doing here?" His own voice was an urgent whisper. "Has something happened to Miranda?"

"Naw, naught that I know."

Callum swallowed his dislike for this man and, with as much dignity as he could, rose to his own feet, snatching his robe from the foot of the bed. They were very much of a height and would have made well-matched opponents. "What do you want of me then?"

"I want nothin'," Wilfred replied, his voice thick and surly. "Ah'v come here to offer my help."

Heaven save us, the man is drunk! Callum thought, noticing his sour breath for the first time. He drew in his own breath, working for patience. "Please explain to me what you mean."

Without further invitation his visitor sat on the edge of the bed and began.

"I know you be somm'at more than ye appear to be. I know you've been meeting with the constable ever since my lad was found dead."

Heaven preserve us, does the entire town know as much?

"I want those men caught. Seems to me that won't be an easy matter, so I've come to offer me help."

"In what way, exactly?" Callum's amazement was growing by the minute.

"What is it they want? I can help them—or pretend to help them."

"Are you out of your mind?"

The lines around Wilfred's mouth tightened. "Look, you stubborn Scotsman, I am not a fool, as you think me. I've already laid the groundwork."

Callum began to consider more carefully. "Tell me," he said courteously. "Go on, I'm listening."

As Wilfred recounted what had taken place at the Napoleon that evening, Callum was more than a little astonished. He had surely underestimated Miranda's father, at least in some ways. "Have you thought this thing through?" he asked.

"I b'lieve so," came the reply.

"You will be placing yourself in the gravest of danger."

"That be not such a rare or a terrible thing."

Strange, strange man! Callum rocked back on his heels. "It could be done. It could be our one best shot, actually. But Mr. Symons, believe me, it will not be easy to carry this off."

"I have enough hatred and anger built up inside me to impress the most dubious among them, b'lieve me, sir. Nor shall I flinch or panic when the going gets rough—I've never once in me life done that."

"I believe you." Callum's mind was racing.

"So, you gain their trust and bargain—for a price, mind you—to take them where they're wanting to go."

The older man nodded.

"But, where is that?" Callum's voice rose in frustration.

"So, who be you anyway, professor? I b'lieve it's time you told me."

Callum hesitated.

"My Miranda knows, don't she? I've seen it in her eyes when she looks at you; aye, sir, I be cannier than you give me credit for."

"All right." Callum sat in the one chair the room boasted, and told the tall, angular man all that had taken place since he found Sammy Tableer's body in the Thames and first encountered his daughter, cowering alone in an apartment and contriving flimsy excuses for her presence there.

Wilfred listened with his brow creased in concentration and, from time to time, a look of distress—wild as the uncharted moors, wild as the sea he had lived his days on—flickered to life in his eyes.

"The girl has too much of her mother in her," he muttered. "Takin' the poor boy's burdens upon her young back. It be not her place!"

Callum drew a deep breath. "That isn't what she was told."

"What be your meaning, man?" The strong forehead clouded and the inscrutable eyes grew dark.

"I have it on good authority—and that is all I will say of it!—that her mother passed the responsibility to her at the time she died."

"I wouldn't disbelieve that; not for a second." Wilfred cursed under his breath for a bit, then resumed his listening attitude. Callum spared him nothing and, when he was finished, the man stood and stretched to his full height.

"I will tell you one thing, Inspector, there be no way this side of hell for us to find Stephyn's hiding place."

"That's what I've been afraid of."

"Oh, I do suppose we could stumble upon it by sheer accident, or the providence of heaven. But there be literally thousands of caves and hollows up and down this stretch of coast—not to speak of the moors, which be just as endless a wilderness. If we had but a clue what he and that Frenchman had done with the filthy goods."

Callum thought the man's description an apt one, and let it go. "What if you pick a spot, good and isolated, and not easy to get to? We can set it up as a trap. That's all we'd need, I believe, to finger them." Callum's eyes smouldered with suppressed excitement. "We could even plant a few 'goods' there, something to tempt them—make it appear legitimate—at least for a brief space of time. We'd need that."

Wilfred considered; Callum, watching, did not like the look that came into his eyes.

"Listen, Symons, I must have your word, your most solemn word on this. If you try anything foolish you will ruin the whole operation, and give yourself no chance at all."

"I understand ye. And you and I best not appear too friendly, not before anyone's eyes."

"Miranda?"

"She must know nothing, you hear me? 'Twould be too dangerous for her. I want to lead those jackals off her scent."

"I agree, but—"

"Aye, she will think even worse of me, and curse my callous black heart. But the lass has despised me these many years, and with good cause. A little longer won't make much difference, here or there."

Callum did not know what to say. He was seeing a facet of this man he had not believed existed, and he was having a bit of trouble coming to grips with it.

"You report to me daily," he demanded, as Wilfred Symons moved toward the door.

"And how do I do that? What time and place?"

"Here, any time after eleven. I'll leave this lamp by the window burning until I'm in the room, and all's safe and ready for you. When it goes out, that's your signal."

"As you will, Inspector."

"Watch that; I must always be Mr. Forsyth to you."

"Have no fear of that."

"I have fear of this whole scheme, especially if I let myself think on it."

"Then, put your mind at rest. I be not the kind to turn back once I've started." The steel eyes bored into Callum's. "I will not fail you, Mr. Forsyth. So lay down on that bed there and get you some rest."

He quit the room as silently as he had entered, but his presence still vibrated, like a force beyond reason, but as real as the sunlight filtering in through Bessie's lace curtains.

Callum stretched out on top of the bedcovers, his mind too agitated for sleep. His instincts told him this was the answer he had been searching for. Yet, at the same time, it was risky, and very unorthodox. He closed his eyes, just to rest them, and realized with a start that Symons had not given his word when he asked for it. "Canny old sea dog," he muttered. "He worked his way out of that!"

But the realization made him uneasy, for he knew he had authorized, and therefore unleashed, a turbulent man whose strengths ran cold and deep, and whose will, iron hard and seasoned, was absolute.

Chapter Twelve

"You think it is fine, Francis? It be not you my father shames with his loose disgraceful talk; to think he would malign poor Stephyn even now . . . even now." Miranda could not go on. Her bottom lip began to tremble and she put her hand to her mouth.

Francis had a quiet voice, but deep and full for one so slender. He used it to try and soothe her. "Miranda, he is more distraught than he wants to show; perhaps this is his way of striking out at the pain. He means no hurt by it."

"I do not believe that. How convenient for him to be absolved of the responsibility of his actions, when no one else is."

"He is to be pitied, not hated."

She opened her mouth to protest, but the words her father spoke at the graveyard flashed into her mind. *I loved her. And I was fool enough to let her love me—and waste her young life for my sake and his.*

She had never before in her life heard her father speak in that manner. Perhaps—far more than she realized—he felt guilty for everything: the death of both the innocent girls he had married, the misery and failure of his only son. *But where does that leave me?* her heart cried. *He turns inward upon his own pain, and I am left to stand or fall as I will. He has never given me the strength and gentleness I long for.*

Francis, watching the struggle reflected across her features, extended a long arm and drew her close to him. "I know he has failed you, Miranda. I cannot even imagine a strength such as you must possess! But his days are used up in suffering and bitterness, and your whole life is before you." He hesitated, considering. "And you do have me to help you—if you'll let me."

He spoke the words simply, not wishing to alarm her. But she only relaxed further into the warmth of his arms, and a fierce longing to protect her from the evil and danger that threatened washed over him with the shock of a cold wave at sea. *She trusts me,* he thought. *If aught happens to her!*

She raised her head, with its weight of fawn brown hair. Her eyes were wet, but gentle. "You do make a difference. You always have, Francis, and even more now. But your tenderness cannot substitute for my father's. My loneliness, my need for him is a separate thing—a void no one else can fill."

The truth of her guileless words was frustrating. "But in time—"

She pressed her finger to his lips. "You need not fash yourself, Francis. I know what you mean, and I know what you feel—and I thank you for it."

He could ask for no more, not at present. He walked with her down the steep embankment of Fore Street and over the humped bridge to the center of town, and left her at the inn shop with a terrible feeling of reluctance. But he kissed her cheek as he left and, with his eyes, tried to express all the things she would not yet allow him to say.

༄

The big American car had disappeared. Since the night Callum followed its tracks to Tintagel, it had never been spotted again. True, the tyre marks on Bodmin Moor had corresponded, so he could assume that was evidence that the same car, and the same men, were still active, still nearby. Indeed, Wilfred Symon's description of the stranger at the Napoleon matched other descriptions, and the name he gave to the Cornishman, strange enough, was his own. *Gordon Willis*—why would he reveal to the father of the murdered boy his real identity? That had stuck in Callum's craw ever since he arose that morning and began to think over last night's strange events.

Unless . . . unless, vague ideas were floating inside his head, but he had yet to pin them down. Perhaps a little help at this point would be in order.

He let himself into Bessie's private parlor, which she had now given him carte blanche permission to use, and rang up the commissioner's office. After detailing the events of the last hours as thoroughly as he thought necessary, he stated his request.

"Have you any men you can spare for a special detail?"

"Let's have it."

"I'd like someone to find out where Rodney Basset is and shadow his every movement."

"Can be done, though it shan't be easy."

"Well, that's not all."

"Go on."

"I want the same thing done with Gordon Willis."

"I thought Willis was taking a vacation in Cornwall."

"I'm not entirely certain about that. See if he shows up anywhere else, will you? It could be very important."

"We'll do our best. I'll put some good men on it."

"Thank you. I hope to make it worth your while, sir."

"See that you do, my man, see that you do."

༄

Callum returned to the lobby of the Harbour Light just in time to catch a glimpse of Francis Callaway crossing the street and disappearing into a small carpenter's shop attached to the ale house directly across the way. He followed slowly and loitered about the entrance in the pale autumn sun, rocking back on his heels and mulling over the events of the past three weeks. So much had happened, and yet he seemed to have made so little ground. Yet he felt, with that itching premonition he had come to recognize, that the balance—which he always pictured as huge scales holding evil on one side and good on the other—was about to shift and change.

At last Francis reappeared and Callum called out a pleasant remark to him, which the young man returned.

"I've something I'd like to show you, professor," he said amiably, "might prove of interest to you."

They walked down the long, open footpath beside the Valency, which was rising in its banks daily and moving sturdily, steadily toward open sea. Not until they turned the wide curve of the cliff that hid them from general view did Callum ask, "Catch me up, lad."

"I've noticed no strangers, nothing untoward, and have been with Miranda almost constantly, save when she be working or sleeping."

"How are her spirits?"

"Boiling like the sea in a storm after the way her dad's been behaving. Have you heard about that?"

Callum wrinkled his brow in apparent concern. "I've heard some," he admitted. 'Tis a pity he causes her such distress."

"Well, he may not be the only one. I've been thinking this last little while about what's going on here."

"How do you mean?"

"'Tis well and good that I intend to protect her, but my constant attentions in a place as small as Boscastle will be interpreted only one way. Especially since I've been dizzy over the lass since she was a child."

"And what's wrong with that?"

"Only the danger of hurting her. Think it through a bit, man. Will she believe I am courting her just because it's my job, my assignment to keep her from harm?"

"Miranda? I hardly think so."

Francis grinned lopsidedly. "With all due respect, sir, you aren't married, are you?"

Callum winced inwardly, but responded calmly. "Not these many years since my young wife died."

Francis drew in his breath and his eyes softened by way of sympathy, but he went on with his argument. "The sincerity, the spontaneity will never be whole in her mind. She'll wonder if this be the thing that pushed me into a courtship, and question my sincerity."

"Och, lad, you're more daft over her than I thought! Don't worry yourself so. The girl has a good heart and a quick comprehension—"

"But I do not want her to feel cheated, not in any way."

The tenderness in the sturdy young seaman reached out to Callum. He put his hand on the lad's lean, muscled arm. "And the carpenter's shop?"

"I need a cover, don't I? A legitimate reason to be hangin' round a bit, rather than spending my time in my boat."

"I'm buildin' a shed for my old dad 'fore the winter sets in." He grinned sheepishly. "Everyone knows he's been after me to do it for years. Ah've told a few, casually, that I tore some ligaments in my leg and the doctor told me the uneven footing in the boat, and the rocking, and the moisture of the sea air would do it no good. So, here I be, doin' a good turn instead, and following Miranda around like a puppy dog."

Callum was impressed. "You've got quite a head on your shoulders," he praised. "I shan't worry about you from now on."

But that wasn't exactly true. He was uneasy at pulling inexperienced civilians into this mess. At first he had thought it both wise and clever. Now the risks seemed to rise to their proper proportions, and he realized he had no real right to endanger their safety, or even their peace.

Peace. That brought him back to his reasons for making

those original decisions. There would be no peace here until he cleared out this nest of vipers. And the police crawling over the town and the countryside would only force them to dig in deeper, or to melt away until things were good and quiet and they could begin their work once again.

So. They were caught between the tide and the shore, the whole lot of them. Yet, the responsibility for the all was ultimately his. He felt the weight of it as he walked back to the inn, bending the strength of his shoulders and making him feel old in a way he had not yet experienced.

Women, he thought. *What odd effects they have upon the inner life of a man.* Laura Poulson and her daughter, Penny, had first awakened this—what would one call it?—vulnerability within him. Painful, to be sure, yet it seemed to enhance his vision, color all things with a richness that had been missing before. He sighed, then straightened his back and quickened his step a bit. *You are doing altogether too much musing!* he scolded himself. He was not used to that kind of thinking; his mind was usually sharp and deductive, and devoid of the messiness emotion brings.

Ah, well. Life was never meant to be static. And it was true, these last days he had felt deeply, intensely alive.

༶

It was Mr. Pascal, the constable, who brought the bag of Stephyn's things to her father's house, but it was she who received them. Francis had brought her home after her shift at the inn shop had ended, and she had fixed lunch for both of them. Francis was strangely attentive these days. She had to nearly plead to convince him that she wanted to take a nap, and that she wouldn't go off anywhere without telling him first. Of course, his concern for her right now was only natural. But she was glad he had not been with her when the constable came. She sat alone in the silence working up the nerve to go through the things, to touch and handle these pathetic remnants of a soul who had flown—of a brief life whose troubled hour was over.

Do not get morbid! she told herself. She had such a tendency to do that where Stephyn was concerned. Perhaps it was because his very birth and existence, his survival—snatched from the grasping hands of the other world—and now even his death were all shrouded with mystery and the white-hot knife of emotions that trembled like heat waves long after the source had sunk beneath the screen of dense darkness, and was gone.

His death seemed so senseless, as though all the struggles of the two women who had loved him were now in vain. A piteous hopelessness ran through her whenever she thought of him now. She sat a long time fighting it, trying to regain her image of him—the real person who had been both generous and tender with her—who gave as often as he took, encouraging her girlish daydreams, and never laughing at her doubts or her fears.

At last she opened the bag and drew each item out carefully. So little here; so little left! There were clothes in his room still, and things he had left there when he first started running; some of his personal books, a model of a four-master their grandfather had carved for him, and a few war medals and momentos arranged carefully along a low shelf. And two photos: one of his mother holding him when he was an infant, her quiet eyes glowing; the other of her mother, laughing and playing with him when he was a sturdy, grinning youngster down by the sea.

There were tears in her eyes now, and she brushed them away with a trembling hand. "What have we?" she mumbled aloud. A change of clothes and a blanket he had taken to the hut with him, a hat, a pair of boots, a small wind-up alarm clock, a stout candle in a pewter holder, one book about the history of maritime warfare, and a few papers.

She thumbed through these aimlessly. Some were receipts for petrol or food, one or two were letters addressed to him. *I ought to give these to the inspector,* she thought to herself. She hadn't the heart to open and read them right now.

She reached for the book and it slid off the pillow where she had laid it, so that the cover fell open. She picked it up by the binding, and a letter fell out, and landed noiselessly on the rug at her feet. She stared at it for a moment. Only one word was written on the plain white surface: her name—in small letters down in the corner; and the envelope was sealed.

At last she bent slowly and picked it up with two fingers, almost as if the touch of the paper would scorch her. She knew instinctively that he had written it for this moment—written it for her to look at after he was dead!

She held it; slender and nearly weightless. Once she slit the seal and opened it, some things would change irrevocably. Knowing this, she hesitated, even entertained the idea of destroying unopened this silent messenger from the grave. In the end she tore at it clumsily and drew out the sheet with an eagerness she could not account for.

Miranda, my dearest, it began. *If you ever read the words written here, then I shall be dead. I shall have gambled for something good, and lost.* . . .

"Something good . . ." Whatever could he be speaking of?

. . . It is true that I allowed Jean to talk me into involvements I did not understand, and now bitterly regret. . . .

Miranda shuddered, thinking of their last talk together, and the fear she had seen in his eyes.

. . . But there is more than contraband at stake here. There is blackmail and perjury, and wicked men preying on those who cannot defend themselves; and the reputation of a good man jeopardized. . . .

Miranda ran her hand over her eyes. Her head ached with the effort of trying to comprehend the words she was reading; trying to find meanings which were only hinted at.

. . . It is my hope to effect my own terms and work some good from this great mess. But, if I am denied that, I shall be all the better for trying—no matter what fate awaits me. . . .

She was clenching the paper so tightly that her knuckles were white, and she let out a small cry as she skimmed the last words and saw that the sentence was unfinished.

. . . If all goes well I shall see you in person, and this letter not be needed. I leave soon for a final meeting and a possible arr—

Miranda crumpled the paper and crushed the ball with her fist, trembling with the agonized frustration which swept through her. "For what purpose?" she cried aloud. "This is worthless, Stephyn; worthless!" Then she bent over, rested her head on her knees, and wept.

෴

After long minutes she roused herself. *Francis will return,* she thought hazily. *I must be gone before he tries to stop me.*

She stuffed the contents of the bag back, tossing the crumpled letter in with them, slipped out the back door and took a long, circuitous route to the center of town, disappearing down alleys and narrow wynds 'til she reached the back entrance of the Harbour Light and flung the door open, sending the inspector staggering.

"Mr. MacGregor!" she gasped. "Did I hurt you?"

Callum rubbed a red spot on his forehead. "Not enough to matter. Has the De'il himself been chasing you?"

He spoke the words like a banter, but his eyes were intent on her face.

"I came to see you," she replied bluntly. "And no one is chasing me, save the shade of my dead brother."

She flung the bag onto Bessie's kitchen table and stood glaring at Callum, her hands planted defiantly on her hips. When he made no reply, but only gazed intently back at her, she spat out like a cornered cat, "I am sick to death of this matter! I want no more to do with it, do you hear me!" She was fairly shouting now. She took a step away from the inspector's searching eyes. "You take the whole lot of it and burn it, as far as I care. And I don't want to see you—or anything to do with Stephyn—ever again in my life."

Her fingers were on the handle and she was halfway through the doorway before Callum recovered himself and made a grab for her, catching only a fistful of her skirt in his fingers. She whirled back to face him. "I mean it, Mr. MacGregor! Just leave me alone!"

The cold vehemence of her voice startled Callum anew. He opened his hand, making no attempt to stay her. It was mid-afternoon, as safe a time as any, he reasoned, watching her shape flit like a shadow and become lost behind a curve of dark houses. "Nor could the very devil keep pace with that girl, the temper she's in now," he muttered.

Nevertheless, he felt uneasy as he turned back to the table and dumped the contents of the burlap bag onto the Formica surface. Common, ordinary items all. He noticed at once the crumpled letter, picked it up and smoothed it as best he could, reading the words quickly and getting the gist of the message before sitting down and considering the whole thing more carefully.

The one word that jumped out as though it were written in bold print was the good old Scots word *blackmail*. The stern line of his jaw tightened. *Reputation of a good man jeopardized . . . gambled for something good . . . final meeting . . . reputation of a good man . . .*

Here was the deeper reason, then, that Stephyn had held out for! Poor young wretch, thinking he could undo evil by dealing with the very men who took such delight in it. A self-styled Robin Hood, scrambling at the same time to regain his own tarnished honor.

The unfinished sentence haunted Callum as he gazed at the words, wrinkled into squiggles and creases by Miranda's angry hand. *Final meeting . . . a good man jeopardized by blackmail*. There was something here beyond the underhanded trading of drug lords with one another. *Blackmail. Someone of note—with money and influence—who had something to hide.*

Callum paced the floor, his thoughts forming vaguely and slowly. He had a hunch or two he would like to follow. He knew, though he dreaded the prospect, that it would be best for him to go back to London himself.

The jangle of the telephone startled him out of his concentration. He ran to get it before Bessie was alerted.

"Forsyth, Francis Callaway here," the voice said. "I'm calling from Miranda's house. She's nowhere about; I've searched the house and the neighborhood. Have you, by chance, seen her?"

"I have. And not by chance." Callum caught the young man's audible sigh of relief while he felt his own throat constricting. "She came to see me on purpose, and she was quite distraught, Francis. But she led me to assume that she was going straight home."

Callum felt the tension crackle over the silent wires, and fought the first teasings of panic he felt building within his own chest.

"I'll search the old ruins and some of—"

"No," Callum interrupted. "She won't be anywhere right now that reminds her of Stephyn. Trust me in this," he said, as his listener began to protest. "Just get down here to the Harbour Light as quickly as you can. I'll be waiting outside."

The receiver clicked and went dead before Callum had finished his sentence. Moving quickly himself, he ran Stephyn's things up to his room, grabbed his jacket, and locked the door behind him, then slipped out the back door and walked cautiously round to the front.

A chill wind was moving in off the sea. The stir of it gave him an uneasy feeling, so that he experienced an almost boyish relief when he saw the tall, purposeful figure of Francis Callaway moving toward him down the long narrow street.

Chapter Thirteen

She had meant to go home, but the idea of being so confined in her present state of mind was untenable. She headed instead for the high open country above the town, where none but the fleetest of foot and most sturdy of intentions wandered. She had never come here with Stephyn, but had wandered all weathers alone, since she was a very young child. *The steep rocks of the cliff are to the girl like the jagged reefs and shoals of the sea are to the fearless sailor,* her father would say. *Those with wildness in their souls must find their own way of dealing with the pain of it,* her mother would always reply. And, as Miranda grew older, she noticed the strange look in her eyes when she spoke the quiet, familiar words.

She refused to stop long enough to face the emotions that seethed within her. She had been docile and obedient and patient for so very long; it was as though something inside her had snapped at the strain of it. *Fear*—fear had been her undoing, more even than pain. It had been wrenching enough to bury Stephyn that night in the cemetery. Why must these few words resurrect the sadness and horror, the terrible waste?

She moved up the steep slope at a punishing rate, so that the cold air burned in her lungs, the sharp sensation serving as a partial pacifier. She was past crying. There was a darkness in her, an anger against her brother that frightened her, and thus drove her on. She did not see the man in the three-piece suit step out to follow her. She did not see the sailor plant his tall, substantial bulk in front of the stranger to block his way.

"Mr. Willis!" Wilfred Symons watched his daughter's ascending figure from the corner of his eye. "We two be well met." He grinned at the smaller man who ground his teeth in frustration. "Might I have a word or two with 'ee now?"

With only the thinnest veneer of courtesy Mr. Willis complied and followed the dour, hard-muscled seaman down to the pier, where the stink of fish and stagnant sea water tortured his nostrils, and the wet sand clung to his polished shoes.

༄

Callum labored up the cliff beside Francis, inwardly cursing the unconscious ease of the young, who were largely unaware of their short-lived but splendid advantage, until they began to be smitten with the lack of it, as Callum was now. Francis was thoroughly unaware of anything but the girl he was seeking, his every sense tuned to her, as keenly as an animal's.

"If she is truly up here, and has a head start on us—" he muttered darkly.

"She will stop some time. We'll follow her down the other side, if we must, lad."

Francis laughed shortly. "There is no simple 'other side,' as you put it, sir, only circuitous trails that grow more and more precarious."

Callum coughed into his hand to cover the consternation the boy's words brought. "I believe she is here, and I believe we will find her," he replied simply. "Have you any better suggestions?"

Francis did not, so they continued on in silence, while the worrisome wind fretted around them.

Miranda heard them long before they came within sight of her. She paused and listened to the scattering of small pebbles some careless foot had dislodged on the path. From a high vantage point above the trail she watched them approaching and, with a sudden burst of mischief, quickly gathered handfuls of hawthorne berries and sent the small, hard missiles raining down upon the startled travelers, giggling unrestrainedly at their confusion and alarm.

"You have come to protect me, is it—the both of you together?" she laughed, stepping out to greet them. Francis lowered his head, his face warm with frustration, but Callum growled back at her.

"If it be good sport to abuse your friends, missy, then, by all means, laugh on." But one sight of her face made him grin, despite himself. And when he recalled her words: *I want no part of anything to do with Stephyn!* he realized how beneficial her harmless tirade was.

"So you've the better of us, and we'll no live long enough to forget it, will we?" he conceded.

"You ditched me," Francis complained sheepishly.

"I had my reasons," the girl replied, glancing at Callum.

"Aye, could you bear with me a bit, lass, and let me explain what I found?"

Miranda nodded and settled herself onto a flat rock, the anger within her receding as gently as the tide at its ebb.

Choosing his words carefully, Callum explained what meaning he had taken from Stephyn's terse sentences. Francis listened, but he kept his eyes on Miranda; great, quiet eyes filled with compassion.

"So I must to London," Callum concluded, "though I am loath to leave you two here at a time like this."

Miranda shrugged. "Might they have simply given up by now? Surely they must have considered the fact that this stash may not be found."

"And give up?" Callum arched an eyebrow. "That would be nice."

"If you could really do it . . . locate the person they're blackmailing . . ." Francis began uncertainly.

"That would be sufficient to nail them!" Callum's deep voice resonated against the black rocks, trembling into a stillness that only the wind disturbed.

Miranda rose and dusted off her skirt. "When will you come back?" she asked, and her voice was as soft and vulnerable as a child's voice.

"As soon as I can," Callum replied shakily, then took the opening, slender as it was. "Will you let this lad watch over you, Miranda, during the time that I'm gone?"

Her smooth brow creased into a scowl. But before she could protest Callum moved close to her and caught up her small cold hands. "I am the one responsible for you," he said, "and all of Scotland Yard knows it. I would never, never forgive myself if anything—"

"All right," she conceded. "Francis is not such bad company." She gave him a small, lopsided smile and gently dislodged Callum's hold. "I am going home now," she said. "Are you coming, Francis?"

The young man threw a glance in Callum's direction, then moved to stand beside Miranda. She slipped her arm through his and smiled from beneath lowered eyelids. *She's still playing with the both of us*, Callum thought. *But this is better, much better, than how she was behaving before.*

He turned to retrace his own steps, while the two headed off at an angle. He felt strangely hollow, depleted. He had gone only a few yards when he heard her voice calling after him; he paused and turned around.

"Take care of yourself, MacGregor. I'm counting on you to come back and finish this business, you know."

He felt foolishly warmed by her words, by the concern her light banter masked. He doffed his cap to her, and turned again to the darkening hillside and the steeply descending path.

~

The drive to London seemed tedious and the landscape more featureless and dreary the closer Callum's approach. He had informed Commissioner Howe of his plans and received a hearty approval. But he could not work up much enthusiasm within himself. Raymond Pascal, the bushy little constable from Tintagel, was now in charge. But his skills and abilities in some crucial areas were scarcely more than token, as Callum well knew. He could trust Francis to keep a level head and judge clearly. But then there was Wilfred Symons to be considered. Perhaps it had been unwise in the first place to give him the green light. Callum felt as though he had scattered the precious contents of a vial upon the sands, the liquid running in half a dozen different directions beyond his control.

I'm overreacting, he scolded himself. *This is what comes of allowing myself to become personally involved in the case. Perhaps London—a perspective from some distance—will actually help clear my head a bit.* He would certainly be grateful if it turned out that way.

"*You and I can hope,*" old Morris May had said. "*There be no harm in that.*" Callum considered the words and the meaning behind them as he drove alone through the long silent stretches of countryside.

༺

After Wilfred Symons waylaid the stranger he manipulated him down the long causeway that led to the pier where a dozen or more fishing boats rested at their moorings. Two or three locals, working about the place, looked askance at the obvious intrusion, but Wilfred paid them no heed. He had decided to continue his blunt, forthright approach: the angry, surly seaman, a little unsettled upstairs since the death of his son; easy to make use of if we promise him something out of the deal for himself.

"Yonder girl," he began, "can be of scant use to you. She loved the lad as only a devoted sister can, and she's a bundle of nerves now . . ." He spat a stream of tobacco juice so close to the gentleman's shoes that he involuntarily drew back his feet. "Naw, she knows nothing. But meself, on the other hand . . ." He squinted his flint-hard eyes and stared at the thin, narrow face before him. "I know the cliffs and caverns hereabouts as few do; these many years the sea has been both bride and nursemaid to those of us who love her." He chuckled low in his throat. "The Cornish coast between Bude and St. Ives is as familiar to me as the back of my hand."

He watched his words take their effect on his listener, and was not unhappy when a boy arrived, running and breathless, with a message that the stranger was wanted to answer a phone call back at his inn. *Takes patience to land the big ones,* Wilfred thought to himself, as he watched the stranger scramble up the hillside. *Doesn't do to play your line out at the first nibble.*

He waited until the figures of boy and man disappeared over the rise, then bent to the workbench spread with tools and an odd assortment of fishhooks and bait and bits of worn netting. If he was going to be taking his boat out, as he suspected he might, there was work aplenty that he must complete first. *Hard work and good luck*—he needed a fair smattering of both right now; either one without the other would not be enough.

୬੭

How could he have forgotten how much he loved the smell and feel of the Thames? Callum rose early, falling into the familiar routine of his life as though he had never been gone. He left Kensington and made his way down to the river, walking the length of the great slate-colored monster from Westminster to Blackfriar Bridge, past the London and Tower bridges to where the wharves and warehouses, masts and derricks mingled their smells with those of the water; and Cornwall did not exist. He could contain all before him as surely as if he were able to reach out and grasp it within one hand. The dark rolling moors, the gray rolling ocean; both had somehow eluded his grasp.

He walked to his office and sat at his desk, poring over lists of fashionable doctors who catered to heroin users, comparing it to a companion list of the wealthy and fashionable—the city's VIP's—who had been marked as known drug users. In this "Octopus Age" as the Twenties were being popularly called, everything was expanding and leveling out, so that the refinements, the finer distinctions of life, seemed to disappear. Nothing was "wrong" as long as it was considered popular, accepted, and the "anything goes" philosophy had become out of hand.

"Poor dupes," Thomas Howe said, coming up behind him. "Bored and rich, and willing to try anything for the thrill of it."

"Never understood that, sir."

"Of course you don't, MacGregor! A good book, soft music playing in the background, and you're content."

Callum scowled. "Ye make me sound as dull and impassive as an old man in his dotage!"

"Nonsense, MacGregor! You take offense at the strangest things." He clapped Callum on the back with his small, nervous hand. "Have you come up with anything yet, my friend?"

Callum tapped the dull lead point of his pencil against the paper. "None of these names will do," he confessed.

"Don't fit your notion?" Howe rubbed at his bald pate vigorously.

"That's right. I am thinking it has to be someone very much in the public eye . . ."

"And?" The commissioner was watching Callum closely.

"For want of a better term, someone with a 'noble' image—a person Stephyn would believe to be worth saving! Otherwise, why would he even care? Why would he hazard so much and convince himself that in aiding this man he would also be vindicating his own past mistakes?"

Howe nodded slowly.

"There is one doctor I know of whose name is not on this list." Callum tapped with his pencil again. "I believe I'll begin with—her."

Howe raised a curious eyebrow, but said nothing.

Callum shook his head. "This calls for an unmarked car and a tweed jacket . . ."

"And the utmost discretion."

"Do not concern yourself, sir. I am not of a mind to do anything rash."

"Well, then, best of luck to you, my man."

Callum pushed his chair back and rose. "I'll report first thing in the morning," he said, biting his tongue on the words he might have added: *earlier, if need be.* He was just superstitious enough in nature to wish to avoid tempting the fates with any overt discussion of either the good or the bad of what might be waiting for him.

༈

Please don't talk about me when I'm gone . . . no matter how I carry on . . . The song danced over the radio waves. Callum, watching the dark street from his dark car, thought of the contrast between the flamboyant, fun-crazed youth the Twenties had spawned, and the quiet, gentle-eyed young woman in Cornwall, who lived and dressed and thought much like her mothers and grandmothers before her for generations had done.

It was a long wait, and the nagging thought that it might be a futile one ate into Callum's brain like the stabbing pain of a toothache. *Wimpole Street*—the heartland of London's expensive medical fraternity—at two o'clock in the morning was as still as a gilt-covered coffin. Callum fidgeted, and tried to shift his feet in the confines of the car interior. The muscles of his legs were twitching from fatigue. He rested his head on the back of the seat and studied the pattern of the fabric on the roof above him until the dim lines became hazy and hard to define.

※

He awoke without realizing, for a moment, where he was, or that he had been sleeping at all. When he checked his watch and saw that it was quarter of five in the morning, a hot sense of shame surged through him, and he cursed himself for the stupid fool that he was. "*Aye to eild, but never to wit,*" he muttered, which was the old Scots way of describing a man who grows older, but no wiser with age! *I should take up crossword puzzles or poetry writing,* he thought—*something to keep me occupied if I can't stay awake by me'self.*

Well, the harm was done now. If anything happened, he had slept like a baby straight through it. He reached to turn the key in the ignition when he saw a shiny black limousine round the corner of Wimpole Street, pulling to rest at the curb where the shadows of several large plane trees nearly obscured it from view.

Every sense in Callum's body was alive now. He sat bolt upright, glad for the darkness of early morning which still obscured him, as well. He did not have long to wait. In less than ten minutes the door to Lady Sanbourne's surgery opened and a tall, slender man slipped out, well-wrapped in scarf and gloves and a long, dark-colored top coat, his averted face largely concealed by the brim of his silk derby. In a moment he would reach the safe anonymity of the waiting automobile, and be gone.

Callum tapped against the window glass with the hard rim of his ring. In the silence it rang like a gunshot. The gentleman's head shot up, only for a moment—but Callum had seen the high straight forehead and the long handlebar mustache that framed the thin mouth.

With recognition, a sick feeling came over him, and he let the quiet car slide out into the empty street and nearly disappear before he turned on his engine and inched out of his parking slot to follow. He must keep as great a distance as he dared, anyway; for this time of the morning, how many cars were abroad? The sound had alerted them; so would a following vehicle. Callum chuckled under his breath, despite himself, when the yellow glow of a street lamp revealed that the license plate ahead of him had been draped with black cloth.

He eased his foot off the accelerator. It was not really necessary to follow the long black car home. He would go back to his own place, bathe and dress carefully, and then call discreetly upon the brilliant, ill-fated Lord Marwood, who had long been a highly respected member of Parliament, and would soon be standing for re-election again.

❧

The man known as Gordon Willis settled himself as comfortably as he could on a large, flat rock, partially sheltered from the wind by a squat, stunted pine tree. From under his beetled brow he scrutinized the Cornishman carefully. *Could the man be trusted? Was he the genuine article?* These were vital questions only Willis himself could decide.

Haven't a lot of options, he thought. *If we had, we wouldn't be sitting here, out in this raw weather making deals with a bitter old fisherman who doesn't know his head from a hole in the ground.*

"What's in it for you?" he asked suddenly, his voice as scathing as his gaze. "Come, man, you want something, or you would not be here."

"Right you are there," Wilfred Symons responded slowly. "I be telling you from the start what it is that I want."

Willis's short blond hairs bristled at the crude response, but he managed to ignore it, so that the man had to add, "I want security for the days when I can no longer work the sea as I have all me life. Whatever it is of yours that my son had is of no more use to me hidden from the light of day than it is to yourselves."

Willis's eyes said, *Go on,* and after a little awkward shifting, Symons continued. "I 'ave my price, and I want you to sign your name as a guarantee to it."

Willis laughed deep in his throat. "This is a matter of mutual trust—nothing more. You must understand that."

"The devil himself has a hard time getting Gordon here to sign on the dotted line," his companion quipped, receiving a sharp jab in the ribs from Willis for his cleverness.

Symons frowned in turn. "It be two against one. Once we're out in that cave, what guarantee have I that you won't leave me there a corpse, and take off with the whole lot yourselves?"

Willis bit at his thin bottom lip. He was growing impatient. "When we meet to do the deed, I'll bring a first payment—in cash. You can keep it on your person, hide it in the boathouse, in a hole in the rock—whatever pleases you. How will that be?"

Symons nodded slowly, and just as deliberately rose to his feet, extending his large, calloused hand toward his slender companion.

"You believe you can deliver?" the thin man responded, keeping his own hands neatly folded in his lap.

"I know every spot along this coast Stephyn might have frequented. If anyone can find what you're looking for, Mr. Willis, I can."

Willis stood at last and put out his own hand, reluctantly. "This be the most binding of contracts, gentlemen," Wilfred Symons said, forcing both men to shake hands with him, and enjoying the discomfort he saw in their eyes.

At the bottom of the slope he parted from the two and made his way toward his own house, feeling a stirring sense of excitement not unlike that he experienced when he was preparing to go out on a particularly dangerous run. *Man against the elements,* he thought. *Man pitting his wits against the wits of his adversary—a process as ancient and essential as existence itself.*

"Lena," he said aloud, "heaven knows I've failed you enough in the past, but I shan't fail you this time."

The wind was silent; he could sense no answer in the stillness around him. He had felt her displeasure that night in the cemetery; he had thought he heard the two sisters weeping together. He knew as sure as he breathed that he must one day answer to both of them for the fate of his son. He accepted that. And for the first time he felt his blood quicken at the thought of what lay ahead.

༄

The two men lingered after the Cornishman lumbered away from them. "Time has run out on us," Willis hissed at his companion.

"I know. I'm gettin' the willies hangin' around here. I swear I can see you know who's face every place I look." Rodney Bassett's cheek muscles twitched, as though his own words had spooked him.

"Butch and Jack should be here by tomorrow night. I'd like to make our move then. Meanwhile—" the blond man rubbed his thin hands together, "we've a little unfinished business to wrap up."

The face before him remained clouded and stupid.

"The girl! We'd be fools if we didn't make use of her."

There was still no comprehension in the face of his listener, but a lurid interest began to flicker behind the brown eyes. "What you got in mind?"

Willis's cold eyes hardened into bits of blue flint. "Something sweet, very sweet. I'll tell you when we get back to the room. I don't trust this place."

"You think the rocks have ears, boss?" Bassett grinned.

"Yes, I think the rocks have ears, Rodney! Let's go."

The two men, mere shadows against the mammoth expanse of the hillside, made their way along the darkening passage to where the pulsing lights of Boscastle waited below.

Chapter Fourteen

This was an estate, not a house. The gate Callum entered opened onto a long drive which may as well have been in Devonshire as in London. There were woods all about; old woods, with a sense of timelessness and peace that made Callum feel like an intruder, knowing the errand he was bent upon. He had gained admittance only on the strength of the commissioner's personal phone call. Now he wished that Howe had come with him; or perhaps in his stead.

He eased his foot off the accelerator. He was in a poor frame of mind to handle the encounter he would be facing. *Take it slow,* he cautioned himself. *When you step out of this car you've got to be somebody to reckon with; a man of parts—a man whose very presence excites respect.*

He thought a bit whimsically of Lord Forbes, the earl of Seafield and Lochmont, a role he had played with some brilliance, if he did say so himself. He thought of the two American women who had so graciously forgiven his gentle deceit. *Laura Poulson.* He would very much like to know what that lady was doing right now. He began to feel a bit better, a bit more whole inside himself. As the Magnette rolled to a stop on the wide curve of gravel, the massive door opened and a smartly-uniformed valet stood waiting as Callum let himself out and approached the entrance.

"Lord Marwood is expecting you, sir," the man said, his eyes slightly averted. "Would you like me to take you in to him now?"

"Yes, thank you."

"Very good, sir. If you will follow me, please."

Callum followed, through the cavernous marble-floored entrance chamber and down a surprisingly narrow hallway to a low oaken door, which the valet opened with a practiced turn of his wrist, pushing the heavy wood inward and standing aside to let the inspector pass. The square study was paneled in strips of rich oak. Large overstuffed chairs sat at comfortable angles to conversation tables that were piled deep with books. George Marwood was seated behind a large library table, trying very hard to appear busily preoccupied. But his eyes, when he glanced reluctantly at Callum, were dull with a sick misery which he could not possibly hide.

He nodded; the valet silently withdrew, and Callum pulled out a chair.

"This may appear an awkward meeting to you, sir," he began, "but I am come as an ally."

Marwood raised an eyebrow; his angular face lengthened and his mustache quivered. "Of precisely what do you speak, man?"

Callum leaned a bit forward, placing his hat and one elbow on the table. "Respect me and yourself, sir, enough to attempt no games with me." His voice was a bit gruffer than he had intended. "I speak of your addiction to heroin, of your frequent, furtive visits to Lady Sanbourne—"

Lord Marwood made one last attempt, drawing himself up and blustering with assumed shock at the nerve of the officer before him. Callum waited patiently, then continued in his same direct manner. "I realize the distress and embarrassment this must—"

"No, you do not! Do not presume, sir!"

Callum ignored the outburst. But his voice when he replied was flint-edged. "I do know that you are being blackmailed, that many precious things have already been extorted from you; that you are prey to some very powerful and unprincipled men." He furrowed the line of his own dark brows, forcing the gentleman to look at him. "And I know that a young man—a foolish, largely innocent youth, was murdered because he attempted to help you."

Marwood was paying attention at last. His skin looked as pale as parchment and the lines around his mouth made his whole face appear tired. "What do you want of me?" he asked. "I have no way to help you."

"I believe I can help you," Callum responded.

Marwood shook his head. "You fellows at Scotland Yard have a great habit of meddling, and nine times out of ten you merely make matters worse."

Callum was losing his patience. "I want a list of the valuables you have given over to these extortioners."

"To what purpose?"

"Sir." Callum moved his chair closer, so that his face was only inches from Lord Marwood's. "I happen to have great respect for you and the work you do. I cannot countenance your weak habits, but that is really none of my business."

Marwood leaned back, away from the unrelenting eyes. "That is neither here nor there, is it? I am not interested in your opinions."

Callum ignored the sarcasm, which he knew was egged on by fear. "I am providing you with a preface of sorts merely to let you see where I am coming from—and where I hope to go with this thing."

Hope dim as the last star of morning throbbed in the weary eyes.

"What we need from you can be achieved in the most discreet, private manner."

Marwood wanted to believe what he was hearing. For the first time Callum leaned back in his chair. "I shall explain the whole thing to you, sir," he said, "with as much dispatch as possible, and then let you judge for yourself."

༄

Miranda paid it little mind when the drunken man

stumbled against her, nearly upsetting her balance and enveloping her with his stale breath as he tried to apologize. It was a bit early in the day for such behavior, but the man appeared harmless, and she went on her way without any further annoyance. Francis was working on the construction of his father's shed, as the weather this day had turned dry and fine. Miranda was glad for a bit of time on her own; since Mr. MacGregor's return to London the lad had stayed at her side like a shadow. And she knew, with a certain irritation, what the worst of that was! She enjoyed his company; she was not tiring of him as she had thought that she might. The feeling alarmed her at times, and far back in her mind she wondered if she was not afraid of marriage, after what her aunt and mother had known. Francis was forcing an issue she had not even thought of before this time of turmoil and tragedy.

She walked home from the Harbour Light at a slow pace, enjoying the gentle warmth of the sun shining on her hair and her face. The sea was quiet, but she could still smell and sense it. Strange, how to seafaring men like her father, the ocean took on one meaning, while to her it had quite another. She neither disliked nor mistrusted it, as Stephyn had. The ancient mystery, as powerful as the tides, as sweet as the crested curl of green foam when the water crawled like a sigh up the stretch of dry sand—these things entranced her, wove a spell she gave way to willingly. Of course, at times the darkness would come crashing; storms and battered ships, and terrified men lifting their anguished cries heavenward. Then the black tales of piracy, the stories of mermaids and silkies and sirens rode on the very spray that the black water churned. Yet, she could not fear it, for it was part of her; someplace deep inside the most ancient part of herself moved with the deep, ceaseless rhythms of the sea.

She was surprised to hear the telephone jangling as she walked into the house, and caught it up on the fifth ring, curious as to what voice she would hear on the other end. She had not expected mystery and the dredgings up of sorrow.

"Miss, this be a friend here. I know sommat that would help you clear your dead brother's name."

Miranda was still. The words sat like stones on her heart, and she felt her pulse race.

"I mean it. I wouldna' be daft enough to ring you up otherwise! Do you want what I have for you, or no?"

"Where are you calling from? Just what do you want of me?"

"Nothin', girl, but to do you a favor!"

The voice on the line was offended, and Miranda felt a sudden panic that the girl might hang up. "You are calling from—"

"Plymouth. Can you meet me at Swan's Fish 'n Chips? It's there on the right just after you pull into town."

"Well, I . . ."

"Can you or can't you? 'Tis that simple."

It would be less than an hour by car from Boscastle to Plymouth, and Francis had left his old car parked back by the shed.

"I'll be there," Miranda replied. "But you had better be leveling with me."

"Come and see for yourself." There was a sneer in the voice that chilled Miranda's blood. "I'll be there in forty-five minutes waitin', but I won't wait for long."

There was a click and the phone line went dead. Miranda did not let herself think. There was no time for anything but the clearest and quickest of action. She did not realize, as she grabbed her purse and sweater and hurried out to the car, how good it felt just to be doing something. Somewhere on the A30 between Eglos and Launceston, she realized that she had not left a note for either her father or Francis.

Oh well, she thought, *Francis will work straight through until nightfall, as long as he has a sliver of light left to see. And my father*—she blinked her eyes at the image of his face that rose before her—*he has been spending less and less time at home since Stephyn's death; he most probably will not even notice that I've gone anywhere until I get back.*

She turned right onto the A384, which would take her straight into Tavistock and, in a further fifteen minutes, Plymouth itself. Her stomach ached with the nervous excitement that coursed through her. *Only a few more minutes,* she thought. *This has to be worth it! I have to have made the right choice.*

～

Howe tapped the edge of the paper against the desk. His eyes sparkled with open pleasure. "A full statement signed by Lord Marwood himself. How did you effect it, my man?"

"I believe he was relieved, sir, to share the burden, so to speak."

"Well, we have two of our best men detailed to him, night and day."

Callum nodded. "We'll need the best, sir."

It was a tight plan, he believed. The undercover officers would pose as Marwood's driver and valet. They were well-trained, and they would be armed. Just in case. The house and grounds would be guarded by a further detail of plainclothes inspectors. At present no one knew of the great man's involvement with the Yard. And, if they could keep it that way . . .

"I've something else for you, MacGregor."

Callum looked up, expectant.

"Gordon Willis has been positively identified—close range—by two separate agents."

Callum felt the blood drain from his face. "How recently? When?"

"Once day before yesterday; once late last night."

"Could he possibly have known of my presence in Cornwall?" Callum mused aloud. "Might he have followed me here?"

Howe's gnome brow crinkled as he watched the inspector.

"Either that, or my hunch all along has been right."

"If this man in Cornwall who calls himself Willis is, in truth, Neville Logan mascarading as his rival, you cannot go back alone, MacGregor." His friend's failure to respond irked the commissioner. "We have Marwood's statement; we can pick Willis up and book him."

"We need *evidence!* Put a canny tail on him and give me a few days. All the other vultures will scatter and fade into the mist if we alert them by arresting Willis."

"I know that. But at least we'd have something, my man. And, in truth, I am growing tired of this game you are playing."

"Aye, nor do I blame you a bit, sir." Callum ran his hand through his thick dark hair, and Howe could feel the spark of his pent-up energy and frustration.

"Let me hand-pick four lads, see if you can clear them—"

"And hold them in readiness, twiddling their thumbs?" Thomas Howe knew his man well. "For how long?"

"Three days at the most; that is all I ask. Maybe less, maybe only a matter of hours."

Howe pressed his white, compact hands together. "Two days, that's all. Then I send them, MacGregor, whether you ask me or not."

Callum winced. He knew when acquiescence was the better part of wisdom. "I'll check in first thing in the morning and then be off. I'd like to get a head start"—he grinned lopsidedly—"on my two days of grace."

Howe ignored the unveiled jibe. "Very good, MacGregor. See you fiveish?"

Callum swallowed and nodded. "Give me twenty minutes, sir, and I'll have that list of names on your desk."

"Right."

The police commissioner bounced out of the room, moving swiftly and roundly on the balls of his feet, and Callum closed his eyes, bringing to mind the faces of men he knew and trusted, men he would want right beside him when a tight moment came.

✧

Miranda found the fish and chips shop easily, slowed the car and pulled it into the gravel parking lot that stood on the side. The place looked deserted, but then, it was three in the afternoon, right between the dinner and the supper rush. All the better. Whatever this girl had to say, Miranda would prefer it to be as discreet as possible.

She pushed the door open and stood looking around for a moment. Two men, well-dressed, with hats, sat in a corner booth, a lone fishwife, with small squinty eyes and florid cheeks took up one whole side of another booth. The voice Miranda heard over the telephone could not have been hers.

She took a few hesitant steps forward. As she did so the two men rose in unison and moved in her direction, stopping only when they were close enough that the taller one's leg brushed against her skirt.

"Miranda Symons?" he asked, in a polite tone.

Miranda nodded. "Yes, I'm looking—how did you know me?"

Both men smiled, and she felt suddenly sick to her stomach.

"We are police officers, miss. We have received a report—"

He hesitated, and the other picked up the thread of his speech in a smooth, practiced manner. "We'd like to take you in for some questioning, if you would oblige us."

Miranda took a step backward. The fear within her was real now, and she knew fear, in these men's eyes, would be construed only one way. "You have no reason to question me, sir. I have no idea—"

The young man behind the counter was leaning forward conspicuously to listen, his morbid curiosity greater than his sense of decency.

"All right. Let's compromise a little. We'll just search your purse and your pockets right here. How's that?"

Miranda felt herself relax a little. Perhaps the girl who phoned her had been in touch with the police and they spooked her into thinking that the dead man's sister might as easily be suspect, be an unreliable character.

The tall man began a meticulous search of the contents of her pocketbook, pulling at the silken lining with his narrow fingertips. It reminded her of London, and the sickening sensation returned to her insides again.

The second man had turned the left pocket of her jacket inside out. Now his fingers plunged into the right one. He gave a little grunt of obvious pleasure as he pulled out a small white packet. "These are the goods, all right." He held it up to the light. "Quarter of an ounce of pure heroin, I'd guess."

Nothing registered. The probing fingers returned and drew out a small slip of paper, folded in half. After the officer read it he turned dark eyes on Miranda. "What does it say?" she gasped.

The man made a harsh sound, far back in his throat. "You'll have to come with us now, miss," he replied; his voice, his whole manner was altered. Miranda felt as though a strong hand was tightening around her throat, constricting her breath.

"Miss Symons, we are arresting you for possession of heroin and on suspicion of drug use"—he hesitated slightly—"and blackmail."

The words were sounds, only meaningless sounds in her ears, like the muted roar of the sea, like the thin wind in the branches of the shivering pine trees that edged her father's yard.

"Miss Symons."

The taller of the two men took her arm, and she let him lead her. She could not resist. She could not even comprehend what was happening. She went without seeing, without feeling that her feet even touched the ground.

۶

"There be enough moon to see by."

"That sliver?"

Wilfred Symons nodded. "I've some torches as well. And a couple extra slickers—" He glanced at the pale men who stood stiffly, expectantly—"just in case the sea plays any tricks on us."

"Just so long as you don't try to play any tricks," the scruffy man growled. Wilfred did not deign to look at him, or give any other response.

They were silent as they climbed into the small boat, so that the slap of the water against the curved sides was clearly audible. The man Willis called Rodney turned his collar up to protect his bare neck. Wilfred bent low and in one fluid movement pulled the engine, the gray waters around them, the whole gathering night into life.

"Where you s'pos'ed to put your legs?" Rodney complained. But even Gordon Willis ignored him. He was leaning forward, watching the prow cut through the thick water. Every now and then his eyes shifted to the quiet, nearly expressionless face of the seaman, whose narrow gaze was fixed on the long, jagged line of black rocks that broke up the shoreline and etched themselves in harsh patterns against the soft dove surface of sea and sky.

Chapter Fifteen

The voice coming over the telephone was more miserable than it was apologetic. "In truth, sir, I cannot find either one of them."

Callum checked the urge to curse the young fellow roundly. "They were merely looking for their chance with her, lad," he growled.

He could almost feel Francis tremble. "I've no idea where she might be."

"Well, I have a good idea where her father is!"

Only silence greeted him, then a reluctant, "Aye, I checked to be sure, and his boat is gone." He added quickly, with a pathetic note of hope in his voice, "Might Miranda be with them?"

"No. That is the last thing these fellows would want. If they've any foul play in mind, and I am certain they do, two deaths would be more than twice as sticky, especially when one is a young, innocent girl."

"Good heavens, sir, what have I done? What might have—"

"Calm yourself, Francis. If we follow my theory out a bit, they've done nothing to permanently harm her. I suspect more than anything they wanted to be certain that she was kept out of their way, and ignorant of what was going on," he added.

Nothing could comfort or even reconcile his tormented and guilt-ridden listener. Callum glanced at the old rosewood clock that sat on his mantel. It read ten minutes of ten. He could still in good conscience ring up the commissioner and head for Cornwall this night.

"I'll be there as quickly as I can, lad," he said. "Tell Bessie you've permission to wait in my room for me. But nose around a bit first, will you?"

"Gladly."

"Cautiously, rather than gladly." His stern tone struck home and Francis gave his word with sober gravity.

But Callum did not feel easy when he replaced the receiver. The sooner he was there, the better. But he'd best call Howe before he dressed or packed.

Just as his fingers reached out for the phone it startled him by jangling in a brash, insistent tone. With a sense of misgiving he raised it to his ear.

"Inspector Callum MacGregor?"

"Yes, I am he." He was disturbed with the late caller for not identifying himself. "And who—"

"This is Officer Roger Snow from the Plymouth force, sir."

"Yes?" Callum felt every muscle in his body tense and an almost fluid energy course through his nerves and his veins.

"We've a young lady here—'pologize for ringing you so late—but she's in a bit of a fix, sir, and she . . . well, she claims to know you . . . claims—"

Callum could feel the blood beating against his temples. "What is this young lady's name, Officer?"

"Miranda Symons, she says, from Boscastle. You see, we—"

"I'll be there within two hours. Prepare any documents necessary to have her released to me. I shall—"

"But, you don't understand, sir. She was in possession of narcotics when we picked her up, and though she won't say nothin' we suspect—"

Callum sighed in audible exasperation. "And did you locate this young lady due to a friendly, but anonymous, tip, Mr. Snow?"

"Why, indeed we did, sir. But—"

"This young woman is entirely innocent. She has been

set up by some characters whose names you would recognize. Her life is in danger, and I want her ready to walk out the door with me the moment I show up. Is that clear to you, Officer?"

Only an awkward silence greeted him, so Callum added, with some satisfaction, "I was about to dial the Commissioner of Police when your call came. I shall have him ring your superior, since that appears the only way I shall get any action from you."

He was too angry and too worried to behave in a gracious manner. Before replacing the receiver he added tersely, "You'd best hope, for your own sake, that the young lady has not in any way been misused or mistreated."

He did not wait for the stammered defense that greeted his threat. Even when he got Thomas on the phone his manner was shaken and a bit wild.

"You'll prove your own worse enemy and of no good to the lass, MacGregor, if you continue in this manner," Howe scolded. His reprimand subdued Callum at once. Made him ashamed, actually, of his lack of proper professionalism.

"I shall have your men ready for you." Howe reminded.

Callum thanked him briskly, unable to see the delighted smile that played about the thin mouth as the small, compact man wished him luck and rang off.

Callum sorted and packed his things with a heavy heart, as though a leaden weight sat in his chest. Even his feet felt leaden as he lifted them and walked, with a weary steeling of his energies, out into the night.

The cool air had a certain felicitous affect upon his nerves, and once he was off and driving the terrible tension within him began to lift. It was a good four hours from London to Plymouth, though at this time of night he met no other vehicles on the road in either direction, and felt safe to push his usual limits a bit. There was a slice of moon in the sky, enough to make the landscape feel friendly. Perhaps he ought to have tried to reach Francis before he left. But time wasted at this point would prove counterproductive. At least Miranda was safe. The constriction in his throat relaxed a bit when he considered that in a matter of hours she would be out of harm's way, and under his protection again.

※

This time of year after a certain hour, no matter how fine the day had been, the waters of the Cornish coastline were cold. Wilfred Symons wore a brown leather jerkin and flannel trousers thrust into his sea boots; besides, he was used to such weather, such conditions. The men in the boat beside him shivered beneath the inadequate clothing they wore. Wilfred watched, unmoved. He had taken them out some distance, toward Porth Joke where claws of low black rock curved into the water and a protected cove assured the access he desired. He knew certain of the caves that were carved into those cliffs; the one he had specifically in mind was shallow and narrow and seemed to end in a disappointing pile of shale, layered and overlaid, that concealed a low, ragged entrance leading back to a series of caves: tall, dry caverns that doubled upon one another until they led back to the sea.

He beached the small craft where the line of water meeting sand was too black for any but his eyes to see. It took very little time for him to feel in the darkness for the wires he had placed, and connect them to certain points on the engine after he had shut her off. Only a few extra seconds—but the next time she throttled into life promised a right blazing show of fireworks.

Wilfred set his teeth for the ordeal ahead. "I've checked the smaller caves closer by," he explained, as he gave each man in turn his hand and helped him from the rocking boat to the solid shore. "Seal Hole was a favorite of Stephyn's."

Rodney Basset grunted as he followed unsteadily in the dusky glow of the torch trained at Wilfred's feet. The sea smell was strong here, the rancid flavor of unseen things that were rotting. Willis drew out his handkerchief and held it against his nose.

Their guide moved slowly up a beach whose incline was gradual, yet made to appear more steep by the wet sand that clung to one's feet. The dragging pace, the inky blackness that pressed outside the torch's glow, the unfamiliar night sounds, all combined to put the strangers on edge. Wilfred Symons knew that; indeed, he was counting on it.

The sound of the water that followed them seemed louder once they entered the rock enclosure. The walls, dripping and indistinct, appeared to tremble with the force of the water that troubled them.

Willis grabbed the torch from the fisherman's hands and played it wildly around the cave. "There's nothing here!" he said, through clenched teeth. "What are you up to, old man?"

"You ask me?" Wilfred countered. "Do you b'lieve I'd come all the way out here for nothing?"

It was the uncanny, unexpected combination of sensations—impressions—that altered Wilfred Symons's simple, naive plan. Willis heard a sound—the whine and churn of tons of water chafing against the cage of a sea hole. But he took it for the cry of an engine, seeing himself trapped here, with half a dozen police craft circling the cove. Then Symons shifted his weight and Gordon Willis saw the bulge in his pocket, and jumped to his own conclusions—moving even as the impulses touched his brain like hot wire.

He tore out his own gun and aimed it at the tall figure who, observing the movement, had bent to scoop up a stone which he threw half a second after the shot sounded—the shot that had been meant to enter his chest, but licked like fire into the flesh of his thigh. He made no sound as he fell into the plunging darkness, darkness that rose with the force of a wall to meet their sightless eyes; for the stone, too, had found its mark, and the torch hit the shale floor and shattered as its white eye blinked out.

Rodney Basset swore profusely, cursing everything that came to his panicked mind, starting with his boss's stupidity, until Willis, in the panic of his own terror, turned the gun in his direction and fired two wild, undirected shots.

"I'm getting out of here," he hissed. "If you want to come with me, shut up and get moving."

"What about him?"

Wilfred Symons was already crawling, dragging himself across the cave floor toward the jumble of rock at the back. If he could find the ragged opening and crawl through it, he would be safe. There were more bullets in the gun, and another strong-beamed torch in the boat. If Willis decided to come back with the aid of that light, and finish what he had started . . .

Willis swore graphically at his companion's question and began groping his way back to what he hoped was the mouth of the cave. They had not gone far; sight would have shown him only a few feet's difference between himself and the freedom of the white, open beach. But the long, black minutes it cost him to cover that distance set all his muscles trembling. When he emerged into living air, with the stars overhead, his whole body was covered with sweat. There was nothing here, nothing. His nightmare back in the cave had been only the tortured invention of fear. He stood blinking at the star-bathed silence before him, where the last veins of white froth curled under his shoes.

Rodney had already clambered into the boat. "C'mon," he called, cupping his hands over his mouth. But the sense of urgency had drained out of Gordon Willis.

"Throw me that torch," he cried. "It's somewhere near the middle, under a tarp." As Rodney searched, he added, "Can you start the engine? The key's still in it." He had checked that, to be certain, before he'd climbed out of the boat.

Rodney threw the torch to him in a wide arc. He barely caught it with the tips of four fingers. He moved a few steps closer to the boat, feeling the tide fill his shoes, then wet his cuff, his pants legs. "Count to one hundred, slowly," he instructed, "then start 'er up." The noise of the engine, he reasoned, would cover the sound of any further gunshots.

Rodney, sitting squat on his heels, nodded. As Willis turned away from him he began to count, watching the white head move beneath the white stars. His feet were cold; he never had liked getting his feet wet. He watched and counted until he had reached one hundred and seven— seven, his lucky number. He groped for the key, closed his fingers around it and eased himself into the pilot's seat, foot over the throttle.

Willis was within a yard of the cave mouth when he heard the explosion. It tore through the night like the roar of a thousand sea monsters tearing up the sand, churning the water into tongues of red and green flame. He turned around to watch, still not quite believing. "The sly old fox," he muttered at last—free to indulge himself in a moment of admiration because he was standing there on the high sand, alive and breathing. As he ducked to go through the cave entrance he thought of the pleasure he would have in killing this man, who had proved to be a halfway worthy adversary, after all.

꒒

It had taken Miranda a long while to break out of the stupor that held her. She must have answered a series of questions, perhaps even signed her name to a form. They locked her in a cell, a large cell at the back of the police station. Four iron beds stood in a row, with a mattress and pillow on each of them. Someone brought her a blanket, home-knit of thick, rough wool. She sat on one of the mattresses, her feet dangling over the edge and wrapped the warm blanket around her legs. Someone else brought her a cup of steaming tea. She remembered drinking the tea. But she did not remember curling up like a child on the thin, striped mattress. She did not remember closing her eyes.

When she woke up she was calling his name. "Callum! Callum MacGregor!" Shouting it at the top of her lungs. Someone unlocked the door. Someone led her out into a small room where the glare of the light bulb on the ceiling made her eyes squint and her head ache.

"Call Chief Inspector Callum MacGregor," she demanded, "Scotland Yard, Thames division." From the expressions on the startled faces around her, she knew they thought she'd gone mad. She drew herself up and took a deep breath. "I have been working with Inspector MacGregor," she said, speaking her words slowly and concisely. "His number is written, in my own hand, in the little leather book in my purse. Go ahead, look for it."

When the tall officer discovered that she was right, he shrugged his shoulders. "Wouldn't hurt to try," he said. "Can't lose nothin' by trying."

"No. Only our jobs if we end up pestering the wrong bloke."

The tall man looked at Miranda. She forced her eyes to meet his; she forced them to remain calm. "Hand me the phone," he said, still watching her. "I'm too curious now to let this thing rest."

༄

It was with no small sense of triumph that she saw Callum enter the room, walk directly to where she was seated, and lower his large bulk down beside her until he sat on his knees, his eyes nearly on a level with hers.

"Are you all right, my dear? Did anyone hurt you, cause you distress or embarrassment?"

She shook her head at him, both angry and amazed that her eyes were filling with tears.

"It's my fault," she said, her voice little more than a

whisper. "I should have known better—I should have at least left a note, I—"

Somehow her head found his shoulder and he was pressing his large, starched handkerchief into her hand. When he arose and turned to face the local officers his square jaw was set, and the glint in his gray eyes all business.

"Which of you takes responsibility for telephoning me in the middle of the night?" he barked.

"I take that responsibility, sir," the tall young officer answered.

"Very good," Callum replied. "Someone was bright enough to act on initiative and instinct." He glanced briefly at Miranda. "Who is the officer responsible for her arrest?"

"That would also be me, sir," the same man replied.

"Roger Snow, is it?" Miranda could tell that Mr. MacGregor was enjoying this. She began to relax a little herself.

Callum drew out pad and paper and made a written note of it, while Roger Snow fidgeted uncomfortably. At length MacGregor folded the sheet and handed it to the young man, who stood watching him nervously. Then he held out his hand to her and she took it, rising, and following the London policeman out into the gray, flat dark of predawn.

Once she was comfortably settled on the passenger side of the Magnette she asked him sleepily, "Did you put in a good word for Roger Snow?"

"Indeed I did. Wrote a recommendation for promotion."

"Good," she sighed. After a few moments of traveling in silence, she sat more upright and addressed him again. "All this was arranged by the same men who killed Stephyn, wasn't it?"

Callum nodded in assent.

"Why Plymouth?"

"Plymouth is a place far enough removed, where you are unknown, where the authorities would be impressed by their own discovery, without knowing any of the particulars of what was happening closer to home."

She leaned forward a bit. "As well as the drugs, there was a note in my pocket. Did you get a look at it?"

He smiled into the darkness. "Of course."

"Well, what did it mean, then? Stephyn was right, wasn't he? These men are blackmailing someone . . . someone with the title of Lord before his proper name."

"Yes," Callum acquiesced. "Yes, Stephyn was right."

She was growing excited now. "What did you discover in London?"

"Things that, with the grace of heaven, will help all of us."

Her eyes bit into him, willing him to say more. But he only patted her hand. "Get some rest now, lass, you may be needing it."

She relaxed back against the comfortable contours of the seat and drew the plaid lap rug MacGregor had given her up over her chilled arms, tucking it under her chin, as a child would.

Callum watched her with a sense of quiet satisfaction. At least he could make some small things right. She closed her eyes, and after a few minutes he could hear her soft, even breathing. He rubbed his hand over the bristle of whiskers at his chin and kept his eyes on the faint black ribbon of road—stretching on, around every curve, over each rise—it kept going and going.

But he was not really seeing it. He was seeing a black stretch of sea, with a small, sweet-crafted boat dipping and rising, dipping and rising, as the cold swells, colliding one with another, rolled and shivered beneath.

Chapter Sixteen

Willis entered the cave with his whole body poised on the sharp-toothed edge of expectancy. He enjoyed the near pain of that sensation. He played the light from the torch over walls and ceiling, then swept every inch of the scaly, uneven floor. He refused to believe the utter emptiness that met him. He repeated the process again.

Rage ran like a poison through his veins, souring anticipation into a seething frustration. It was impossible, considering the facts as he knew them, that Wilfred Symons had disappeared.

"I hit him; I'm just not sure where," Willis muttered aloud. The cave ended, surely, in the back there where the pressed layers of shale stopped it up. Should he check? He walked forward a few yards, then stopped suddenly. He was hearing noises again. What if Symons had run for help? If even now, as he stood here vacillating, people were on their way?

He remained poised, like a well-trained hunter, his mind working cunningly behind the mask of his face. It came to him all at once—like a flash of intuition! He chuckled under his breath.

Most likely, he reasoned to himself, *the fool has crawled away to bleed to death somewhere. As for myself . . . that was one heck of an explosion out there in the cove. Two bad those two stranger fellows were blown into a thousand pieces.*

His body began to tremble with excitement. What better cover than to let everyone think he was dead. Too bad, perhaps, that he had taken on this hated alias. But even that, even that could be worked to advantage.

He moved swiftly now, with the lithe precision of a wild animal who was trained to use all his senses in the interest of self-preservation. As soon as he reached the mouth of the cave he shut off the light. Only now and again, as he climbed a steep, meandering path upward, did he flick it on for brief seconds, to show him the way. There would be a road of some sorts when this hill crested. A village with a chemist where he could purchase the materials he needed to once again alter his looks. But no one must see him while he was yet Gordon Willis. Willis must disappear, all trace of him obliterated beneath the pounding sea waters.

His face was grim as he walked, but his nimble mind was already planning step after step, move after move ahead.

༄

Callum carried Miranda in to her bed and she scarcely aroused herself to notice, stirring only when Francis leaned close and kissed her. He remained in the silent house, while Callum went to beg mercy from Bessie, who agreed to stay with the lass for the rest of the night.

The rest of the night. The pink-edged fingers of morning were already spreading through the gray blanket of sky, soon to disintegrate the mass of night altogether. Callum shuddered, for as he approached the Harbour Light he saw the form of Constable Pascal approaching him.

"Just got a call from the coast guard," he reported, as soon as he came within earshot. "An explosion's been reported off Porth Joke; exact whereabouts still uncertain." He scratched at his full cheek, where a mass of hairs curled.

"I'd like to investigate myself," Callum replied. "Would that be possible?"

Pascal considered. "I don't see why not."

"Francis Callaway here has a boat," Callum observed.

"That he does, an' he's as good a pilot as any."

It was agreed that Francis would take them out, but using one of the coast guard vessels, which was larger and well supplied for any possible kind of emergency.

The preparations seemed tedious and annoying to Callum. Perhaps, he wondered afterward, perhaps something within him had sensed the inevitable because he felt no surprise, not even a burst of annoyance, when he looked up and saw Miranda standing like a slim shadow outlined in white sunlight on the pier.

Francis glanced from the girl to Callum and back again. At last he said, with as much firmness as he could muster, "You are not coming, Miranda. Will you please go back to the house?"

She ignored him and addressed her next words to the inspector, whose eyes were still on her face.

"I dreamt of my mother," she said simply. "I never dream of my mother. And the dream woke me up."

"It's your father," Callum replied. "There was an explosion at Porth Joke. We think it was your father's boat."

"My father is not dead."

"Do you think, if you come along, you can prove that?"

Miranda stepped down into the boat. Callum reached out and touched her arm briefly, then returned to his duties. Francis stood gaping at her, feeling his own awkwardness.

"I owe you an apology, Francis," she said, still in that voice that had no more life than a morning shadow, yet carried the timbre of echoes and memories, and frightened cries in the night.

"I was worried sick for you," he replied. "You could have trusted me."

"It was nothing like that." She looked into his eyes, trying to instill some of her calm there. "It was my stupidity, my own blindness."

The boat was humming; she had not heard the engine start. They began to move out from the shore, and she turned her sea eyes seaward.

Francis sidled close to Callum. "She's one of the ghosts herself this morning," he tested.

"Yes," the inspector responded. "I believe you have something there."

༞

They headed straight for Seal Hole Cave. "It was one of Stephyn's favorites," Miranda said. "My father would have taken them there."

"Do you believe it holds the treasure?" Callum asked. But at first she would not answer, turning her withering anger upon him, for he had been forced to explain, as they moved across the pool-still morning water, what he had allowed her father to do.

"You should know better," she said at first, and he was too kind to remind her that no one said yea or nay to Wilfred Symons. Then, after a few more moments she added, "He will sacrifice himself, you know, after some weird design of his own."

Now only her eyes spoke, until her stubborn pride surfaced and she said, looking at no one in particular, "The 'treasure,' as you put it, will not be in Seal Hole Cave."

And, of course, she was right. They beached the boat in the cove, and were lucky enough to discover a few pieces of wreckage, caught between rocks, or being chewed and tossed by the breakers. Constable Pascal, the fourth member of the party, offered to act as retriever while the others walked up to the cave. Callum carried the extra large torch, official coast guard issue. In a matter of seconds it showed clearly that the cave was as empty and bleached as a skull.

Miranda said nothing. She stood leaning slightly forward, expectancy in every line of her body. When she reached for the torch Callum gave it, and followed her to the very back of the cave.

At first he saw no reason why she should lean down, her

eyes searching the thick darkness along the cave floor, her fingers feeling the seams in the shale, as if the rock might split at her touch. Then his eyes, adjusting, perceived the difference, and he bent down, too, and saw the jagged hole, and shouted for Francis. Miranda wanted to go in herself, but Callum would not allow it. She stood with the taut watchfulness of a young doe, and waited, and Callum waited beside her in the pressing sightlessness, until the yellow beam nearly blinded them as Francis crawled back through.

"He's in there, all right. And he's alive." His voice was husky, and his eyes, when he lifted them to Callum, held a warning.

"Is this a trail of blood?" Miranda asked, stooping to touch with one finger a dark stain in the rock.

Callum didn't believe he could fit through the opening; Miranda slid past both of them at the first sign of the inspector's weakening. She and Francis together managed to get Wilfred to where Callum waited. From there it was easy. They carried him to where the boat waited, laid him on a stretcher, and covered his cold body with blankets. Porth Joke was not far from St. Agnes, where there was a small but adequate hospital. Pascal had the engine going before the injured man was fairly settled.

Miranda knelt at her father's head. But she did not catch his cold hand up in hers, nor smooth back his matted hair, not try to speak to him. Callum would have given a year's pay to know what the lass had in her mind.

༄

MacGregor and the constable, in their official capacities, accompanied her father into emergency. Miranda sat on the grass beside Francis, her legs covered with Callum's plaid rug, waiting.

"Your father's condition is stable, but they will be operating on him," Callum reported as he came out to meet them, "and I have not enough time to wait here."

Miranda lifted her eyes to him. "Do you believe the other men died in the explosion?"

"It would appear so," Callum hedged.

"Then, what work remains for you?"

Callum smiled slowly. "Miranda," he sighed, "will that rich heist remain forever a mystery—a mystery that grows into legend?"

She did not take his words lightly. "Is its discovery that important?"

Callum considered. "It would make everything that much easier. Now we have just so many men's word on the subject, all differing. Drug money is powerful proof in a courtroom—not to mention goods that fall under the heading of extortion."

"But, if this Gordon Willis was one of the worst of them," Francis added, "haven't you achieved at least one grand coup with his death?"

"Mr. MacGregor does not believe that the man called Willis is dead, Francis." Miranda stated the words like a fact and, once spoken, they sounded sane enough.

"It's just a feeling I have. I'm used to paying attention to feelings, especially when there isn't much else."

"If Gordon Willis is alive still, then my father—despite his foolish heroics, despite wiring explosives to his engine—is still in danger."

Callum smiled stiffly. "Aye, my dear, that he be."

"Well, for the time being," Francis shrugged, "the old boy is out of commission, and I suppose your fox's laying low."

"Not necessarily. I believe that time's running out for him. It certainly is for me. I've less than forty-eight hours to bring in something substantial."

"Like a couple of bodies." Francis grimaced.

"That might do for a start."

Pascal came up behind them. "We've plastered Willis's picture everywhere within a hundred mile radius," he beamed. "That ought to help."

"He won't look the same," Miranda said bluntly. "Mac-Gregor knows that."

Pascal bristled a little, not knowing how to reply to her.

"We might flush out more than the one fox we've been following around in circles," Callum added dolefully. "It's time now for that."

He knelt down on the grass beside Miranda. "Francis will stay with you."

She nodded curtly, her eyes on some far-off point, but unfocused.

"Why are you yet so angry with him?" Callum asked softly, under his breath.

"My dad?" she replied, the sounds cold and staccato. "Why shouldn't I be?"

"He risked his life, lass, his credibility and reputation—"

"He did just what he wanted to!" she cried. "Like he always has."

"And this time?" Callum's tired brain was a little bit hazy.

"He wants to die. There is nothing, really, to hold him here."

"Lass," he tried to soothe, "you cannot honestly say that—you cannot truly know."

Her eyes flickered over his, and he saw disappointment reflected there, and somehow her pitiable reckonings made him feel like an old, foolish man.

He walked off with Pascal and left her there, in the circle of her own silence, with a young man bending over her—slender and quiet and confused by the depth of her pain and the force of his love.

ॐ

He refused to stay in the hospital. After they cut the bullet out of his leg, Wilfred demanded to go.

"I got a bed at home better 'n this one," he said, with a wink in the nurse's direction. "Let someone who really needs it make use of this room."

In the end, they released him into the young man's keeping, with a long list of instructions and written prescriptions to fill. When he rolled the papers into a crumpled ball and tossed them into the ocean, Francis glared at him darkly, but his daughter did not attempt to disguise her disgust. "Grow up, Father," she told him. "What good does that do, beyond proving your ignorance?"

He could guess that her meaning extended to the larger experience neither one had yet mentioned. But he would not let her see she had hurt him. "'Tis none of your business," he growled, "what I do."

She bit back the half dozen rejoinders that came to her; she had given up arguing with the man long ago. Perhaps she was being childish still, to expect him to apologize to her; and she knew she was being stubborn to refuse to praise his nerve and courage—proper manly virtues, as far as he was concerned.

She made him take to his bed, as he had promised. Rest was the best thing for healing, and he would give in that far. In truth, the bullet had not gone deep, nor torn through any bones or arteries. He lay awake for a long time, wondering, as Callum was wondering, if Gordon Willis had been killed in the explosion. It seemed likely; yet, somehow he could not believe it.

If the man is alive, he thought, *he'll be back for me. I can't be here when that happens, I can't risk Miranda's safety.*

At last he allowed the muffling gray cotton that was clouding his brain to take over, and let sleep, for a little while, have its grudging dues.

༶

Miranda was tired herself, but she did not want to stay here. "Let me come to your father's with you, Francis. There must be something I can help with."

"You will help by simply being there—with me," he said. His directness, unhampered by an excess of emotion, pleased her. They walked down the steep, friendly streets together, hand in hand, as though they were very young and life had not yet bruised them, or torn its way through their tender defenses.

※

Callum was bogged down by triflings, following every lead, every report that trickled in to the makeshift office he shared with Constable Pascal. He had forgotten how tedious this aspect of police work could be. The only light through the murk was the long shot he had taken, with Howe's permission and cooperation. He had sent flyers, by personal carrier, to be dispersed through all parts of London describing this Gordon Willis and placing a substantial price on his head. He could almost see the commissioner's eyes sparkling at the possibilities that might come from such a bold act.

Meanwhile . . . it was the meanwhile that was telling on Callum. Sometimes he found himself not caring who was caught and who wasn't, as long as this thing got resolved. He wondered if Howe would send his reserve force, as he had promised. He wondered if Wilfred Symons was in danger, and if that danger would spill over to engulf his daughter.

※

It was really by accident that the man called Gordon Willis saw the *Wanted* poster with the blond man's image smirking back at him. He could stand and examine the features at his leisure, for his hair was dyed to a rich shade of brown, so dark it was nearly black. And, with the aid of careful padding, he looked a good thirty pounds heavier than the man in the drawing. A mustache, trim and narrow, sat above his top lip, and wire spectacles, with clear glass lenses, rested low on his nose. He wondered how far abroad these notices would be posted. He wondered if getting to Symons would make any difference now. He wondered how long he would have here on his own before things blew wide open and he would have to take the narrow avenue of escape he had provided for himself.

☙

The gray day diffused into a gray night. Callum sat at the Napoleon with Francis as the long hours dragged, feeling as restless as the great sea that sounded just beneath his consciousness. Miranda had agreed to spend the next few nights with Bessie Youlton. Callum and Francis had escorted the two women to the Symonses' cottage where they prepared a meal for the sick man and gathered some of Miranda's things.

"You stay put here," Callum had cautioned Wilfred. "It's the safest place for you this next little while."

"I'll go daft spending another day in these four walls!" he groaned. "And, what's more, man, I be a sitting duck here. Is that what you want?"

There was no talking to him. Not now, any more than before. Perhaps in some ways Miranda was right.

☙

It was late when the two men shook hands and parted. Callum took his time walking to the Harbour Light. He didn't look forward to being cooped up in his small room at the top of the house. The sky was all stars, stars he couldn't remember seeing since he was a boy in Scotland. He felt encompassed by a universe that took little heed of him. Sea and sky moved to the rhythm of forces far beyond his comprehension. Who could say what existed between earth and heaven? Who could say what the worth of one life was, one human heart?

When he stepped inside, the light in Bessie's parlor seemed glaring and the room stuffy and warm. He was surprised to see Bessie herself curled up in one of the easy chairs waiting for him. "Is it Miranda?" he asked quickly.

"No, the lass be all right. You've had a fellow from London looking for you. Rang up twice during the last hour."

"Why didn't you send someone after me?"

"No one to send. Everyone around here be asleep, including my Frank, and I wasn't about to leave things here unattended."

"You could have awakened him."

"Didn't think of that," she replied.

Callum was irritated, but at the same time amused. No one could move a Cornishman too quickly, especially where he did not want to go.

"Name's there by the telephone," Bessie said, rising. "You be wanting anything else, sir, before I turn in?"

"No thank you, Bessie. Thank you very much for waiting up for me."

She smiled. "No trouble, really. Long as all this is happening, I'm just glad you're here, sir."

Her kind words warmed him. He picked up the paper, recognizing at once the number she had written. He dialed the digits of Thomas Howe's private line with a sudden impatience.

"That you, MacGregor?" the familiar voice said. "About time you came in out of the cold." He chuckled, highly amused, though Callum could not see why. "The bird has flown, my friend."

Callum felt all of his muscles tighten. "You are sure of it?"

"Absolutely. A most reliable source."

"Good." Callum drew a deep breath. "Have you any idea how many friends he brought along to the party?"

"Can't say with any degree of accuracy." Howe chuckled. "But your own friends should show up sometime tomorrow."

"Wonderful. We'll roll out the red carpet. Ought to have a grand time."

"Stop feeling sorry for yourself," Howe barked, but not unkindly. "Have Grant call and report in once they arrive."

"Very good, sir."

Callum rang off. His whole system felt wired, and the current that ran through it was more heady than the finest wine or the richest Cornish ale.

Chapter Seventeen

Miranda slept late. Covered by Bessie's large feather ducat she felt warm and secure for the first time in weeks. After the luxury of a hot bath with Bessie's lavender bubbles, she dressed with care, and felt the nightmare of the last few days falling from her.

It was with a sense of anticipation that she walked out into the morning air, pleased at how mild it was, how warmly the sun shone from a blue, cloudless sky. *The sea will be as blue*, she thought, *with only a few tattered seagulls, or a jaunty sail or two to tell where sea and sky part.*

She found MacGregor and Constable Pascal in the room Bessie had relinquished to them for a temporary office. The inspector looked haggard; even when he lifted his head to smile at her, his eyes, usually so deep and arresting, appeared tired and dull. She wished she could think of something to say, somehow both kind and clever, but she never could at such moments. Instead, she heard herself asking lamely, "Do you know, sir, where Francis is?"

"The lad's running an errand for me, actually." Callum answered. "You look fresh and lovely this morning."

She felt herself color a little as she lowered her eyes. "Might I just go over home and check on Dad, and tidy things up a bit?"

Callum hesitated. "I would feel better if Bessie goes with you."

"I shan't put her out more than she's—"

"Nonsense." Bessie came out from the kitchen, wiping her hands on a tea towel. "It be good for my Frank to discover just how much of the work around here is generally done by me! I'd enjoy the walk, dear, on a morning like this."

They set off together, over the curved bridge, picturesque enough for a postcard, or perhaps the cover of a novel. Callum watched from the window until a large farm cart loaded with hay rumbled on behind them and blocked his view.

He turned too early to observe four men jump from the laden cart and saunter toward the Harbour Light. Four strangers to town, all at once; all together. Their entrance made every head turn, both inside the inn and out on the village street.

"Is that kidney pie I smell?" one asked another.

"I don't know, but this clean country air has certainly got my appetite going."

"Dinner at noon, straight up," Frank grunted as he walked past them.

Callum did not have to turn round to see; he had already recognized one of the voices.

"Your lot may be good on the streets of London, but you stick out like a sore thumb here."

Keith Clark grinned back at him. "The old man said you'd defend your territory like a tenacious terrier. But remember, you asked for us, old man."

"Only in a manner of speaking," Callum lamented. "I was given no choice."

He wanted to laugh at the outlandish costumes the four men had assumed in order to "fit in" with the locals. In truth, he did not mind having them here. If their presence helped wind things up at last, all the better. If warfare broke out between the two power lords and their presence could prevent bloodshed among the innocent townsfolk—he sincerely hoped it would not come to that. When would Willis show up, and would he be bold or cautious? And Logan, with his wiry build and his red hair; would he appear as himself this time or under another disguise?

Bob Grant called the commissioner to report their safe arrival, then Callum appointed each a station in strategic points throughout Boscastle: one to the sea-walk stretching to the shale heights above the harbor; one to start at the Napoleon and make his way from pub to pub, keeping eyes and ears open; the third to float from business to business, looking for the faces he would be able to identify immediately. Clark volunteered for the harbor detail. "I have a little pleasure craft of my own," he explained. "Least I'll be able to carry on some conversation with the fisher folk down there."

After four hours they were all to return and report to Chief Inspector MacGregor at the Harbour Light. All was in order. Now it would be only a matter of waiting, and perhaps being fortunate as to how and when the pieces all fell together; "the luck of the draw," as some called it, and it was an element not to be overlooked.

୰

The day was too fine for staying indoors. Wilfred could smell that when he first awoke, before he drew back the curtains and found his instincts confirmed by the full, yellow light of the sun. Nothing would be better for his sore bones and muscles than sunshine. He ignored the stiffness and the dull pain that came with movement; by this time in his life, he was no stranger to pain. He hobbled down the banked roads to the last bridge, which skirted most of the city where curious eyes and tongues might detain him. He knew in his gut that the man called Gordon Willis was alive still. The realization did not frighten him, but it chilled his insides, despite the warmth of the sun. As Wilfred headed down the curve of the pier, he saw Morris May's familiar round head, framed in a fringe of white hair, as he bent over his work. With a sharp pang the realization struck him: *I no longer have me boat. I be land-bound and homeless.* For indeed, without a vessel, without a means of riding the waves and making a livelihood, life may as well be over and done with, for such as himself.

It might have been worth it if they had both gone down, he thought bitterly. *'Tis this Willis fellow, not his hirelings, who is responsible for my Stephyn's death. And I missed him, missed my one chance of getting him!* It made him feel like a fool to think how he'd botched the matter and lost his boat—for nothing.

He was wincing by the time he reached the end of the pier, and he walked with his shoulders hunched over and his head well down. The few scattered men who were working there knew what this meant, and were inclined to respect it; if a man wished to be left to himself, it was not in their nature to interfere. They gave as much, and would have expected as much from another. The sun beat hot. Wilfred took off his cap and bared his head to it, drinking it in through his pores the way the damp sand did, eager for its cleansing touch.

Gordon Willis was angry; he could not remember being this angry since the time two of his warehouses were mysteriously fired and, in a matter of hours, he lost fifty thousand pounds. No, this was worse. This was not only money out of his pocket, this was a man's pride—a strong man's private identity! He knew Logan was the biggest fish in the pond; he knew the man's intent was to destroy him. But this was going too far! His short blond hairs stood on end at the thought of the confrontation ahead. He welcomed it; let this thing be resolved one way or another—right here and now. He couldn't hold his head up in London, anyway, if it wasn't, so was there really a choice? Even hotshots like Neville Logan could go too far, too far for their own good. He bristled and boasted, stoking up his courage the only way he knew how.

When he arrived in Boscastle he took his two cronies with him and headed down to the pier. He understood some sailor had rented a boat to this man who called himself Willis. Therefore, this would be the first place to start asking questions, shake folks up a little. He had no intention of playing as mild a hand as his imposter had done. He was here to do business; he was here to see action. He was here to make sure there were no doubts as to who the real Gordon Willis was.

༄

Wilfred Symons was scraping barnacles off the hull of Peter Heard's old sloop; a way to keep his hands busy, but nothing too strenuous. He was bent over nearly double when he saw the three men approach. Though the sun was at an angle to blind him, to make the figures shimmer as colorless and one dimensional, he felt goosebumps prickle his flesh and his insides go cold. He knew who the blond one was—the one who moved out ahead of the others, his head tilted at a cocky angle, his eyes as cold as bits of shale broken off the cold mountain. Without changing his position, without scarcely moving, Wilfred laid down the blunt scraper and picked up one of the sharp scaling knives that was resting nearby. The thin, haughty man drew closer. Wilfred watched him from under a lowered brow, his muscles poised and ready, his senses sharpened by the bile of bitterness within him.

Gordon Willis moved closer to the taciturn Cornishman. He could feel the man's distrust, and he experienced a perverse desire to provoke it further. *Here is someone who knows something,* he thought with relish. He walked purposefully, almost tauntingly, until he stood within feet of the stern of the boat. Then, with his right hand, he drew back the front panel of his suit coat to hook his thumb in one of his belt loops.

Wilfred saw the gesture and moved before it was completed, before the bulge at the man's waist—within inches of those long, tapered fingers—could be drawn out and become living fire, as merciless as the fire in the calloused, contemptuous eyes.

The knife moved in a swift, graceful arc, too unexpected for the gaze that watched it to grasp. As it sunk home the muscles in the lean face twitched, then sagged, contorting into awkward, unnatural expressions that ran into one another, until the man himself folded and crumpled, all at once, onto the ground.

In a matter of seconds the men behind him responded. Each drew out his weapon and shot in a random, staccato pattern. Wilfred had ducked inside the hollowed wood cavern for protection. He heard the whine and ping of the bullets as they sang, and then struck. He did not observe the ensuing confusion as Keith Clark vaulted over a sawhorse, aiming his weapon at the larger of the two men, and bringing him down; calling out to the second, shooting after his fleeing figure—cursing his own ineptness as the culprit kept going—then jerking to the ground, his legs buckling beneath him as the man turned and fired one well-aimed bullet at his assailant. He saw none of this; nor did he see Morris May, several feet away and running toward him, freeze suddenly in his tracks, stand stiff and surprised a moment, then topple over heavily and remain still where he lay.

༄

When Callum looked up to see Peter Heard walk into his office, he knew there was trouble. The man's face was ashen—these Cornishmen usually had such closed, quiet faces.

"You'd best come, and quickly, sir. There's been a shooting down at the pier. One of your men, and the white-haired stranger . . . and . . ."

Callum placed his hand heavily on the man's shoulder and shook his head warningly. Miranda and Bessie were just coming through the front door, chatting pleasantly with one another. When Miranda looked over and saw Mr. MacGregor glance at her, she called out, "He isn't at the house, sir. But then, did any of us expect it? Bessie and I cleaned up, washed a few clothes, and left a stew simmering on the back burner."

She continued walking as she spoke. When she entered the room and recognized one of her father's old cronies, her voice dropped an octave, and the words began to come slower, like a record on a Victrola that had wound itself out. "Is my father at the pier?" she asked Peter.

He nodded in her direction.

"Well, is he all right?"

"I b'lieve so, Miss Miranda, but there has been some trouble—"

As soon as Miranda began questioning his visitor, Callum leapt into action, sending Raymond in search of the two London agents who were wandering the town, and Bessie to find old Dr. Teague, who had been retired these ten years or more, but would serve their purposes just fine. He was past the little clutter of people and out the door before they could gather their wits about them. The first to slip after him and follow was Miranda.

She kept her distance, fearful that he would send her back if he saw her. Peter had said her dad was all right. He wasn't lying; she'd have seen that in his eyes. Then why this burning constriction around her heart and middle—this unaccountable sense of sadness?

Peter Heard and Frank Youlton were yards behind Miranda, who had nearly caught up with the inspector, when they reached the end of the pier. But each one liked to tell the story for a long time afterward: tell of the blood-chilling cry (like the lamentation of tortured spirits) that shuddered through Miranda Symons when she saw her grandfather laid out on the ground, of how she sank to her knees beside him and cradled his head in her lap, rocking back and forth, back and forth, crooning the old words to him while she smoothed back his white hair. It was a sight to be remembered a lifetime—poor tormented young thing.

Callum watched Miranda from the corner of his eye while he assessed the damages. Gordon Willis and his big brute of a henchman were both dead. Keith Clark had been hit in the shoulder. Someone had already tied a torn shirt around him to staunch the bleeding; he ought to be all right. Willis's other man had disappeared altogether; and, of course, that was not good.

"Sorry I let that one slip away, sir," Clark apologized through clenched teeth.

Callum gave him a fierce glare. "You were here, Keith. No man I know could have done better."

Callum sat on his heels beside the wounded man. "Tell me about the knife, Keith."

"Symons there threw it. The blond man was striding purposefully toward him, and I suppose there was a pretty evil intent in his eye."

"Did he actually draw on Symons?"

"No. But he pushed his jacket back and appeared as if he were going to." Keith gave a low, involuntary chuckle. "Willis didn't have a chance, MacGregor."

Callum snorted. "I can well imagine," he muttered. He rose and turned reluctantly round to face the mournful trio, feeling himself shrink before the raw, naked sorrow that reached him from where he stood. "You sure about the old man?" he asked Keith Clark.

"I checked him myself, sir. I don't think he ever knew what hit him."

Callum leaned over and patted his friend's shoulder in a gesture of comfort. "Doctor's coming down the causeway; he'll take care of you, Keith. I've got to get that girl out of here."

Callum avoided Wilfred Symons's eyes as he knelt down beside his daughter. "Miranda," he said, touching her gently on the arm. "It is me, MacGregor."

"I know who you are, sir, and what you want of me."

That was all. Beyond that, it appeared, she had chosen to ignore him.

"My dear," he tried, a bit more firmly. "You must come with me now."

She shook her head. "I won't leave him yet, I won't leave him here."

Callum looked round a bit helplessly and saw, with relief, that Francis had returned and been directed to the harbor. He was coming down the causeway as quickly as his long legs would carry him. Behind him came the three London detectives, with Pascal trailing well in the rear.

When Francis came close he sought Callum's eyes for a moment, seeming to grasp at once all that he needed to know. He knelt, too, and drew one of the girl's slender hands into his. "Dear one," he murmured, "where would you like us to take him?"

She glanced up sharply.

"MacGregor and I together can carry him gently enough, Miranda. No one else need be involved."

She sat poised and motionless. Callum could almost see her mind working behind the veil of her sorrow.

"Take him home and lay him on the bed he shared with my grandmother. Can they . . . take care of him there?"

"Yes," Callum answered emphatically. He rose, aware again of the presence of her father, standing but a few feet behind. Francis helped the girl up gently, with his hands at her waist. Then he and Callum bent over and carefully lifted the form of her grandfather, moved to the foot of the deserted causeway, and began their long ascent into Boscastle.

Callum was aware of the pairs of eyes that watched him—bored into the flesh of his back—as he walked away from the scene. He was keenly, painfully aware of one man, who still stood apart, who had not been invited to participate in the ritual–the tender respects being paid to his father-in-law. He stood in the circle of his own misery while Miranda, alone, followed the body of her grandfather, hands folded in front of her, eyes staring straight ahead.

Chapter Eighteen

No one came into or out of Boscastle after that afternoon. Six additional plain-clothes officers were sent from London, four of them to be stationed at Tintagel, which was just minutes away. The main road through town was cordoned off by the police, and no one left or entered without careful interrogation. It was openly known now to all in the village who headed the operation, and Callum was deeply moved when so many of the townspeople approached him shyly to offer their services.

"It be our homes and families that are threatened," Ginger Fry told him. "We want to do our part in this. It be our place, not yours, sir."

Callum was glad of their assistance. He posted townfolk on all the local roads and lanes that crisscrossed the bleak, wild countryside. Even the hillside walks were covered, as well as the harbor entrance, which was easy to watch and control. By the day following the killings they had a smooth-running organization in place.

Callum was not a little surprised to see Wilfred Symons show up at his office mid-morning. He lowered himself stiffly into a chair and came bluntly to the point, as was his way. "The man I killed is not the same one who shot me in the cave."

"I know that, Wilfred. This man was the real Gordon Willis, a powerful underground figure in London."

"And the other'n? The one who killed Stephyn."

"Neville Logan is his name. He was impersonating his rival purposefully, to destroy him and his organization at the same time he was getting something he wanted very badly himself."

Wilfred sat silent, digesting what the inspector had told him. "Logan is a powerful drug-lord, works internationally." "And what does the man really look like?"

"Thin and wiry; taller and leaner than Willis was, actually. Has a fair complexion and red hair."

Wilfred nodded. "He still be around these parts."

"I'm not sure of that. He might have chosen to melt away until things here cool down a bit. After all, the havoc has worked largely to his purposes, hasn't it?"

"What of the stolen goods that are supposed to be hidden here?"

"Maybe he'll cut his losses there, too."

"No, he be here still."

The way Wilfred spoke the words sent an unpleasant shiver along Callum's spine.

"No, I cannot prove it," Wilfred continued, watching Callum's expression. "But I know it be true, just the same."

He rose slowly, and spoke this time without looking at his listener. "It be not your fault. I place no blame on you, sir, for my daughter's behavior; no, nor for her feelings neither. I just want you to know that."

Callum thanked him, or tried to; it was not easy to express warmth to this man who was so strangely contradictory. He limped out of the room, but the uneasiness of his presence lingered, like discordant music, played too low to hear, but not too low for the senses to feel.

※

Callum was a bit surprised, as periodic reports came in throughout the long day. There was no activity; nothing the least bit amiss had been noted. *What can be going on?* he wondered uneasily. *Have things really ground down to a stagnant halt?*

Late in the afternoon the wind shifted and the weather became dirty, with squalls of gray rain blowing in from the sea. Peter Heard's brother, Lewis, came into the office, hat in hand, his face looking tight and drawn.

"Think you ought to come with me, gove'nor, if you don't mind, and see what I've found."

Callum grabbed one of Frank Youlton's slickers and, with Constable Pascal at his heels, followed Louis along the curving, steep path that led down to the sea. As they left the protection of the craggy cliffs and dropped below the outer breakwater, the wind tore at them like some fierce living thing. Callum set his teeth and pushed his hands into his pockets. Through the slant of the thin rain he could see a dark shape stretched like a stain, or a sudden shallow hillock, along the sand. He knew at once; he had seen too many dead bodies not to recognize at once what he saw.

Once they reached the spot Louis Heard stepped aside. Callum bent down and examined the body, turning it half over so he could get a view of the face.

"Stranger," Pascal pronounced smugly.

"Stranger number three," Callum said. "The one who got away from Clark yesterday. There are no bullet holes, no signs of violence." He looked inquisitively at Louis.

"I saw him from the cliffs," he responded. "Up there, where I was patrolling."

"Do you think he fell?"

"I do not, sir. I believe he must have been pushed."

"Why is that?"

"Good solid ground there, nothing to make a man miss his footing or slip; solid ground with a cover of moss and grass, sir," Louis patiently proceeded. "The fellow either jumped of his own accord, or somebody helped him along."

Callum stood upright, brushing his hands together; it was a mark of dismissal as well as anything else. "I believe you are correct, Louis," he replied. "Raymond, can we get somebody down here to remove the body? I'd like an autopsy, just to be certain."

Pascal nodded vigorously.

When they got back to the Harbour Light, Callum rang up the commissioner to catch him up on the latest. "I believe it was the personal work of Neville Logan," he said.

"One last stab before quitting the scene?"

"Maybe."

"No one's shown up yet?"

"Not a sign, not a soul. It's as if Boscastle slid off the bloomin' map and disappeared into the sea."

"Singular," Howe mused.

"They bury the old man tomorrow. Early in the morning. His granddaughter insisted. I'll call you when all that's over, if nothing happens before."

He rang off and sat in the welcome silence for a few moments, staring into the gray day—as forbidding and threatening as all the other forces that surrounded him. He sat thinking, pressing the ends of his fingers against one another, and suddenly he felt keenly alive. The sensation tingled through him with the satisfying strength of a tonic, an elixir. He felt not only capable but willing to face the darkness around him, to do battle against evil in the old, noble sense that his Scottish ancestors had. When the lads traipsed in for their next report, he was ready for them—his eagerness, his confidence like a warmth that infused the room, and rejuvenated the faltering spirits of the cold, tired men.

꒰

Miranda had not expected to grieve like this when her grandfather died. He was an old man who had passed a full and generous life; he was ready to go. What was more, he had buried his wife and two daughters. Surely there was more waiting for him on the other side than there was left to him here.

It is sorry for myself I am feeling, she thought. *He never entertained such weaknesses. He gave freely to all, without stopping to count a person's worthiness. No one could hurt him enough to make him turn selfish and shrunken inside.* Perhaps if it had not happened so quickly, in such a senseless manner. *Had it really been his time to go?* She could wonder and fret herself 'til the sea dried up, but would she have any more answers than she possessed right now?

The colors of the sunrise the morning of her grandfather's burial were watered down and largely obscured by the seeping, pervading gray of the sky. *Oh well, he is not here to care, or to notice the difference.* She dressed for the funeral, aware of how short a time ago she had performed this same ritual. *Is Stephyn here?* she wondered. *Are he and grandfather watching?* She was glad Francis would be there beside her. She did not want to cry. She did not want to shake like a leaf and weep. Her fear was that, if she once started, she would not be able to stop.

༂

The stale cold air in the stone church had chilled Callum to the bone. Out here the trees broke most of the force of the wind. They laid Morris May to rest beside his wife, but the scar of Stephyn's grave, too new to be healed yet, lent an element of tragedy to the scene it might not have otherwise had. He had not really spoken with Miranda since that afternoon when they walked from the pierside; at least she had been in Francis's tender care. Now, again, she was the dominant figure of the scene, standing black as a raven in her mourning, small and grave, like a figure out of a painting depicting years that were past.

These observances, for whose good were they? Surely not the living, he thought, remembering his wife's death and the panic he had felt at the idea of her young, white body being smothered beneath the ground. He shuddered and turned away from the youth and vulnerability which stood before him, and drew forth memories from him which were too painful to face.

※

Miranda had no desire to be cruel to her father. But she felt herself shrink every time she tried to approach him. Now watching him, stiff and gaunt by the graveside, she thought he looked old and weary, very weary.

He remained standing a long time, and she wondered what thoughts might be pressing inside his head. She saw him start, his body jerk briefly, as with some sudden shock, and she glanced quickly around her, wondering what he might have seen. As her eyes moved they encountered the searching gaze of MacGregor, and she knew he had caught instantly her confusion and concern. He began to move slowly toward where she stood with Francis, just a few feet behind her father, who yet remained by the open grave.

As MacGregor approached, her father said, without turning, "Your man, Neville Logan, was here. I did see him there, behind the large yew tree, his greedy eyes boring holes through me."

"What did he look like?"

"Dark hair, with a bit of a mustache, heavy-set. With eyeglass, I do believe he wore eyeglasses."

"You had the sensation he was watching you?"

"I knew it full well, sir. He was here, and to no good end."

Miranda, listening, realized she was clenching Francis's hand with all her strength, her fingernails digging into his flesh. She turned her gaze to her father and saw him glance up and away from them, his face taking on an expression that made her pulse start pounding. She felt the gray, moist air thicken into something akin, loosely akin to a shape. He had seen it, too; her father had seen it before her.

MacGregor, and all else, were forgotten. In the sudden silence they all seemed poised on that indistinct border where two worlds merge and meet one another. The inspector felt it. She saw his eyes question Francis, who bent close to her and whispered, "Is your mother here?"

"I am not sure," she replied, "but I think it is Florence, and I believe she has come for him."

She felt the muscles in the hand she held tighten. "I don't mean in *that way*," she breathed, watching in fascination as her father began to move away from the group.

Mother! her heart cried. *Help me! Do not leave me blind and powerless.*

Wilfred seemed of a sudden vague and preoccupied, almost dreamy. "I be going home now," he stated, to no one in particular. "My leg hurts sore from all this walking and standing about."

Callum watched him limp off, thinking what an odd one he was, when he felt the gentle pressure of Miranda's fingers on his arm.

"My father is not going home," she said. "I think Florence may be taking him down to the pier."

"What in the world!"

Miranda shrugged. "I can see only the faint glow of her, like the faded gold edging of sunlight. But I think . . ." She shrugged again. "Well, it doesn't really matter."

"The devil it doesn't!" Callum growled. How this girl could disconcert him!

She had gently disengaged her hand from Francis's hold. "I'll take you home now," he told her. But she shook her head at him as she slowly backed away.

"Where are you going instead?" Callum asked her.

"To follow me dad for a bit. See what he might be up to."

"You know very well what he might be up to," Callum challenged her. But her expression did not alter, and she did not deign to reply.

"We two are coming with you," Francis asserted.

"Do what you'd like," she replied, and Callum had to bite back the frustrated response that was fairly itching to be spoken.

She walked with quick steps and a sure determination down the steep streets, following the dark flow of the Valency, toward the curved, sunken pier. Once or twice she thought she saw her aunt, moving just ahead of her father, drawing him patiently on. The two men followed; subdued, yet burning with curiosity and the sense of something they could not see or explain.

༶

Morris May's boat was a simple outboard runabout. Wilfred was already maneuvering it into the narrow channel that led out to the sea. He ignored the approach of the three who had followed him. But Miranda walked right up to him.

"Where is she taking you?"

He glanced up, despite himself. "You saw her, too?"

"Not distinctly. It's Florence, isn't it?"

His eyes betrayed the answer she was seeking. "Then, it has something to do with Stephyn."

He was angry that she could expose his secret so easily. "Out of my way, lass," he growled. "I have things I must do."

"Not so quickly." Callum spoke with the full power of his rich, resonant voice. "You can't do this alone, and you know it."

Wilfred lowered his head and tried once again to ignore them.

"Your daughter is part of this. You know she is; you know that is what Florence intended."

Callum's words gave the stubborn man pause, so Francis stepped into the void. "I can pilot her for you," he offered matter-of-factly. "You'll not manage long with that leg of yours."

Callum was reaching the end of his patience. "It be that way, or no way," he said, not noticing the grin on the younger man's face which his choice of words drew.

Wilfred Symons knew he must concede, but he would not do so gracefully. He hauled himself into the boat, refusing aid from anyone. "I be skipper, and none else," he bellowed. "My word be law, once we get out into the waters, and no questions asked."

"That's fair enough," Francis hastened to assure him and, with a look from Miranda, Callum held his peace.

The sea was boiling where the breakers crashed and collided one with another. *Dirty weather for such a venture,* Callum thought, but he kept his thoughts to himself. Francis grabbed some slickers and an extra torch from the small community shed that all the fisherfolk used. Callum sensed that something was afoot here, and he tried to go with it, though he was out of his element. He caught Miranda watching him, and gave her a grim smile.

"Florence will not lead us astray," she said. "You have nothing to fear, Inspector."

He grinned wholeheartedly then, having this chit of a lass tell him his business, and put him to shame! He leaned into the wind as he felt the boat slide beneath him, and drew the pungent, heady flavor of the water into his nostrils, and the eagerness seized him again, to be off and away.

Chapter Nineteen

They headed north, above Boscastle, into the teeth of a squall that lifted the spray and swept it into their faces, drenching them almost at once. White and black: that was all Callum could think of; the white boiling water, the black sky, and the blacker bastions of wet, slanting rock.

Past Rusey Beach and Voter Run they pushed, past the high cliffs where the Strangles spread treacherously, with Sampire Rock above them. Callum could not see Wilfred Symons's face; he could not see how, in these battered cliffs, sheer and rugged, any aperture accessible to humankind could exist. As they approached Crackington Haven the pounding of the seas increased until Callum thought the unbearable sound was the very pulse tearing through his own flesh. When Francis curved and cut the engine to a slow sputter Callum was dumb with amazement. There was no chance of beaching here; no chance of surviving the waves that would splinter them against the spiked cliff edges. He tightened his grip until his knuckles went white. The ragged black crag loomed high above his head, its angular ridges intensifying the ominous crashing of the waves.

As the little vessel nosed headlong into destruction, Callum braced himself for an impact when, at the last moment, a conduit, a silken ribbon of water opened up where no opening could be imagined, and Francis eased the boat into a gentle crawl, coming to rest on a shallow ledge of sand.

They followed Wilfred on stiff, cautious legs. The cavern, like the sea alley, was at first invisible to the most discerning of eyes. Whoever, or whatever, was directing the old fisherman drew the little group into the blackness, as solid as a wall before them. But it, too, opened up into a low, half-moon entrance which they stooped to pass through, single file. Here in the dimness which even the torches could scarcely penetrate, the roar of the sea was louder and ominous, like some living, breathing essence, bellowing with hostility.

Wilfred moved slowly, but surely, through the first large cavern which sloped into a low, cramped passageway which Callum did not relish passing through. As he brought up the rear, he was the last to step into the smaller chamber, softened by a graceful curved ceiling of creamy stone, streaked with rich shades of blue and yellow. He saw a light as he entered, which, he tried to convince himself, must be the diffused, grainy glow of the torch, insubstantial and weak. Miranda was watching the light, her face calm and composed, but her eyes fever-bright.

Callum heard Francis gasp and followed the younger man's gaze to see a long, broad table spread with stacks of money—crisp, neatly piled bills, hundreds of them. At the farthest end were arranged a sampling of fine art treasures: oil paintings, silver candelabra, rare books, fine Lemoge china and rare, oversized Staffordshire spaniels; heirlooms missing from the house of Lord Marwood, if not others besides.

Callum moved closer. The abundance here was something worth finding, worth taking risks for. *How had those two young men managed to abduct it all and secrete it away?* He shuffled through some of the stacked items, looking for something, with only a hunch to go by. Lying on the top of a stack of old books he spied a small leather-bound volume, slender and pocket-sized, bearing no name or inscription. He picked it up and opened it. Page following page was covered with closely written lists: names, street addresses, and cities. He held it lightly, as though its touch might burn through his flesh. "Francis," he breathed softly, "do you know what this is?"

"Appears like a directory of some sort, sir."

"It is a directory 'of some sort,' all right."

"You look pale, MacGregor," Miranda said, at his elbow. "Are you all right?"

"That I am, lass," he replied. "That I surely am." He smiled at the two confused young people watching him. "What I have here is a rare catalogue of the entire underground operation, across Great Britain and Europe—even into the United States—drug lords, blackmailers, extortionists, forgers and murderers." He glanced at Miranda. "This was the trump card Stephyn held, that made him attempt to work miracles." He sighed. "But, in the end, it was too big for him. In the end, it was what got him killed."

He was concentrating on the images evoked by his own words. He did not even see Wilfred move, until he had clumsily shoved Miranda aside with a jab of his elbow, and somehow worked himself between the two men and the low, shadowed doorway.

"It is not worth getting killed for, Inspector, but so it must also be with yourself."

Callum turned in the direction of the voice to see a man standing just inside the low doorway, a rather lumpy man with dark hair and a mustache, and the silliest wire rimmed glasses perched low on his nose. *Logan—here?* The man's ability to follow—his relentless, almost uncanny pluck—was unnerving, and Callum realized it would have been impossible to hear or see any boat that might have followed them through those high, fermenting seas.

The Ruger Logan held was aimed at Wilfred Symons's forehead, right between his eyes, but Logan glanced quickly at Callum, his lips stretched in a thin, wicked grin. "When the lot of you disappeared—first into the sea, then into the rock—I knew you were going *somewhere*. One inch at a time, the way opened up for me, too."

Logan returned his merciless gaze to the Cornish seaman. "You first," he said through clenched teeth, while an expression of pleasure flickered along the muscles of his face.

Perhaps it was a bat; perhaps it was not; but something swooped down upon him—something alarming enough to cause him to raise his hands in the air. At that moment both

Callum and Francis acted, as if in consort: Francis dove at the man's knees and brought him down to the ground. Callum wrenched the weapon from his hand, twisting the wrist and bringing it down hard across his knee, where he could hear the bones crack.

Tossing the gun to Francis, Callum secured Logan's hands behind him, though the man bellowed protestingly at the pain this caused. Only seconds had passed, but awareness of the triumphant stroke flushed through Callum's brain.

Too late he saw the shadow of a second man moving along the wall to the right of his vision, weapon raised and aimed directly at him. He twisted his body in an attempt to duck away from the coming onslaught, when he saw the large, compact bulk of Wilfred Symons come to stand between himself and the shadow, whose possessor cursed roundly, brandishing his gun threateningly. And, in those few off-balance seconds, Francis lifted the Ruger Callum had handed him, and brought the man down.

The stillness was palpable until Miranda walked carefully, almost cautiously, toward her father and drew him stiffly into her arms. "It will be all right now," she murmured. "They can rest in peace, Dad, and so can we."

There are more mysteries between earth and heaven than men dream of; Callum knew that. What men like to call the sixth sense is perhaps a spiritual capacity we cannot yet explain: more than intuition, less than knowledge; but definitely a grasp of the unknown and inexplicable. He, himself, had seen the ghost—the ethereal essence of Lena May Symons—the night that Stephyn was buried. How could he judge what others may have seen, may have known?

It brought a grim sort of satisfaction to contemplate Neville Logan standing for trial; being held to account for his acts of wanton cruelty and destruction of life; having to accept the just and natural consequences for what he had done.

There was a deep, personal pleasure in reporting this satisfactory, indeed, amazing, conclusion of the case to Commissioner Howe—something Callum had not expected to be able to do.

The London agents moved quickly, and within hours had dozens of astounded angry men in custody. Officials in other key places had been notified; this might well prove a significant haul in recorded criminal history; so Thomas Howe was already predicting, and it pleased Callum immensely to be instrumental in bringing that remarkable man such a coup.

It happened almost too quickly. After the tedious weeks of frustrated blankness, dead ends, and no apparent progress, Callum could not believe the situation was entirely wrapped up and done.

Before quitting Cornwall he had a long list of friends to bid farewell to, and each one was difficult.

"People round here will no forget you," Constable Pascal assured him. "We have long memories, and once a friend, always a friend."

Bessie made quite a fuss of things, hugging him repeatedly, until he was pink with discomfort.

"You watch out for that girl of ours," he exhorted her.

"I understand, sir," she responded. "Miranda will never want for a shoulder to cry on and a warm heart to heed her, not as long as I'm here."

Good people, Callum thought. *Salt of the earth.* He felt himself fortunate to have met them and, in a small way, become part of the ancient rhythm of their lives.

He shared a final few moments at the Napoleon with Wilfred Symons.

"I be grateful to you," the taciturn man said. "If I were locked up—"

"You would not go to jail for going after a character such as Logan—and in self-defense. Put it out of your mind, I tell you."

"It were not Logan, but Willis," Wilfred reminded him. "And it tedn't easy to put out of your mind taking another man's life."

"Aye," Callum agreed, "but one does what one has to. As long as there is evil in the world, that is the way of it." He drew a deep draught from his glass and ventured to add, "You will see to Miranda now, won't you? It is her turn, you know."

Wilfred nodded, though he could not refrain from scowling. "I do reckon you've gained the right to say your mind on the matter."

With those words, Callum knew he had won respect, and an acceptance that would assure him a place here for years to come.

༄

It was Francis who sought him out. "I do believe Miranda will consent to marry me," he said solemnly. "And I know, well . . . she holds you in high regard, sir." Francis hesitated. "It be presuming, I fear; after all, what happened here was a job to you, and you must deal with hundreds of people through the course of your work."

"That I do," Callum agreed. "But only a few who leave a true mark on my life."

At his words Francis ventured to draw a deep breath and continue. "We should like to write, perhaps even visit now and again, sir, and when there are children . . ."

"When there are children," Callum repeated, feeling an awkward tightening in his throat, "I expect to be named godfather to the first—especially if the first be a girl."

A slow grin warmed the young man's lean features. "We be much beholden to you, MacGregor."

"I was doing a job, as you said," Callum answered in a husky voice. "It is I who am beholden, lad, to the lot of you."

༜

He could not find her. Ridiculous as it might seem, Miranda was nowhere around. Perhaps he should not have saved this leavetaking for last, but it seemed only fitting that the business which began with her should end the same way.

Cornwall was cold now, but they told him it seldom grew bitter here. *Harsh,* he thought, *harsh and elemental—the way life ought to be.*

He climbed the long shaled cliff that rose above the harbor, where he had walked with Miranda his first day in Boscastle. Today the sea was not blue, but stained a cold, heavy purple, the weight of it seeming almost to drag down the pale, insubstantial gray sky. She was there. When she looked up and saw him, her eyes softened with pleasure.

"I did not think you would leave without saying good-bye," she smiled, as he drew near.

"Farewell, not good-bye," he replied. "I shall miss you, Miranda."

"Good. Then you shall not forget me."

"No, lass, I shall not forget."

She was nervous, though only her slender hands, fluttering like small birds, betrayed it. "You have done much for me and mine," she said.

"I did not save Stephyn," he answered.

"Oh well, Stephyn was never very fit for this world. He's got both his mothers to fuss over him now, and Grandfather's gentle company. He's better off where he is."

Singular. This down-to-earth faith of the Celts.

"I am sorry, nonetheless." He thought of Wilfred and attempted a smile. "I suppose you feel you got stuck with the short end of the stick."

She understood his meaning, but she shook her head gently. "No, not really. Not anymore. I am glad he was spared."

"A second chance for both of you?"

"Something like that," she smiled, hair and voice like warm honey.

A silence fell, but before it could grow uncomfortable, Callum said, "I've spoken with Francis. He'll make you a good husband, Miranda."

She met his gaze with her own. "Yes, I believe that he will. I am fortunate."

"Yes, lass." Callum's melodic voice softened. "But then, so is he."

Her eyes began to dance. "You would make a good husband, MacGregor."

"I be pretty old and rusty," he grinned. "But I do dearly hope that when I was a husband, I was a decent one."

"Your wife died very young, didn't she?"

"Aye." He wanted to find some way to tell Miranda that he had come to consider her very much like the daughter he never had.

" 'Tis a waste," she said, only half teasing. "A man such as yourself living single."

He thought, unavoidably, of Laura Poulson, of how difficult it had been to say good-bye to her and then get on with his life. "Perhaps you are right," he conceded. "You possess a rare wisdom, Miranda, for one so young."

"That sounds fine," she laughed, "but there is little truth to it." Gulls, as tattered and gray as the ragged sky, swooped low and shivered the air with their plaintive, almost human cries. She pushed a long strand of hair away from her face. "So. You have agreed to be a godfather—in good time." Her fair eyes were dancing again.

"I have not only agreed, but I intend to hold you to it."

She cocked her head, appearing even more comely. "Cornishmen do not forget," she said. "They are much like the Scots in that way."

He sighed. "I must be going, lass." He spoke the words with reluctance. She flitted toward him with the thoughtless grace of a young fairy maiden and stood on tiptoe so that she might be able to wrap her comely arms round his neck. "Haste ye back, MacGregor," she murmured, planting a light, quick kiss on his cheek.

The old Scots farewell nearly undid him. He started down the steep slope of hillside, but after only a few feet turned round and called out to her, "I am glad 'twas me on duty that night in London."

She laughed lightly. "You can truly say so? You must be a glutton for punishment." Then her nut-brown eyes grew serious, took on an almost faraway look. " 'Twas not in our hands," she said, "some higher Fate decreed it."

He looked at her closely for a moment. "I believe you," he said.

He walked down the hill to where the Magnette waited, and took the long straight track north out of Boscastle, choosing the sea road, which was ridiculously out of his way. But he did not have to hug the sharp shoreline to hear the sea calling out to him, with haunting, insistent voices, both old and new. He did not have to see with his own eyes the bleak moors stretch out with the raw newness of earth first created. All was there, scarcely below the conscious level of his mind. He heard with some sense more primitive, more acute, more satisfying than anything he had hitherto experienced . . . indeed, he was to hear the dear, mingling sounds of Cornwall for a long, long time.

About the Author

Susan Evans McCloud's previously published writings include poems, children's books, local newspaper feature articles, narratives for tapes and filmstrips, screenplays, and lyrics—including two hymns found in the 1985 Church hymnbook. The author of many novels, she is listed in several international biographies of writers of distinction.

The author and her husband, James, have six children and four grandchildren. The family resides in Provo, Utah.

Other publications by Susan Evans McCloud:

For Love of Ivy
By All We Hold Dear
Anna
Jennie
Ravenwood
A Face in the Shadows
The Heart That Truly Loves
Who Goes There?
Mormon Girls series
Voices from the Dust
Sunset Across India
Sunset Across the Waters